PUBLISHING

D0169824

Love
By
Chance

Based on the Hallmark Channel Original Movie
Written By Brian L. Ross and Karen Berger

KACY CROSS

Table of Contents

One

SEATTLE IN THE PRE-DAWN HOURS became a misty fairytale place. Claire Michaels loved this time of day, when she could dream the loudest. The light drizzle turned the streets into shiny pathways toward adventure, romance…perhaps heartbreak. But anything was possible. Including a world where Claire owned her own bakery.

How amazing was her life? She'd gotten so lucky to have landed this storefront in the perfect spot north of downtown, near the hospital. Sometimes she had to stop and blink a whole bunch to make sure she wasn't still asleep back in her condo, waiting for all the stars to align before she could gift the residents of Seattle with her desserts on a regular basis.

The bakery was still dark, of course. Her partner Marco wouldn't arrive for a few more hours. Which was fine. It gave Claire a chance to spread out as she created.

She touched the countertop near the ice maker with two fingertips as she passed, a ritual she'd developed. For luck. To assure herself everything hadn't vanished the night before. To bond with the bakery. All of the above.

The pristine white chef's tunic fit like a charm and had only taken three rounds of bleach this time to maintain its brilliance. She'd been sure the balsamic vinegar she'd spilled on the sleeve wouldn't come out. But look what persistence got you. This lovely place. Gilded Sweets Bakery was hers.

Claire flipped on the light and got to work, digging her hands into the almond flour with far more gusto than was probably warranted, but the feel of the cool granules between her fingers had long been one of her favorite parts of the experience. It meant she was in the opening stages of creation, when a new dessert was taking form.

Before long, she had a tray full of lime tarts and chocolate pies that could be wheeled into the cooler while she made the drizzle sauce that would go over the top. And rack. Pour. Separate. Stack. Coconut. Perfection.

Last but not least, she stamped edible gold leaf frosting into the lime coating, dropped more crumbled gold leaf, and topped with a curl of chocolate. Her own recipe and presentation, one that had won awards at a couple of local trade shows. Sure, the accolades were nice. But awards didn't pay the bills, and the party she and Marco were catering that night would.

Some bills, at least.

And, miracle of all miracles, Marco had come into the kitchen at seven-thirty, not quite as dour as usual.

Instead, he glanced up from his bread pan occasionally with a smile that lit up his swarthy Italian features. He was ten years older than Claire with a kind-of lived face that immediately made her feel comfortable with him the first time they'd met.

"I gotta say, those get more and more appealing every time you make them," Marco said.

The compliment pleased her, and she smiled. They hadn't been partners at the bistro all that long, but they'd fallen into an easy rhythm that she appreciated. Nothing about baking was easy, so she'd take it.

"Perfecting the coconut lime tart is an ongoing quest. It's like a triple axel for a skater," Claire said. "You're never sure if you're going to land it."

She backed into the cooler, carefully steering the cart along with her. After investing hours into these little beauties, she couldn't afford an accidental crash. Besides, she didn't want to see her hard work all over the tile floor.

"Well, those win the gold medal." Marco slid the pan of bread into the oven with a rattle that made it sound like the whole contraption would collapse around him—and that could happen any minute now. "When did you get in this morning?"

"Four-thirty," she called from the cooler.

"Why so early?"

That wasn't early. Early would've been three, when she'd actually woken up. "The oven was acting up again. I didn't want to take any chances before the party."

When she came back into the kitchen, Marco's

face had that worried look. The one she'd gotten good at ignoring. Mostly because he'd worn it too often lately.

"Don't start." The finger he pointed in her direction said the same thing as his face. "We can't get a new oven until we get customers."

"If we don't have a functioning oven, we're not going to have any customers at all," she retorted.

This was an argument they'd been having a lot lately. If only there was a good solution that didn't involve donating body parts to science or begging obscure relatives for money. She wanted to do this thing on her own merits anyway, not due to handouts.

And she would. She and Marco had a solid business plan that was taking a while to materialize, that was all.

Marco lifted both hands into the air in his classic dramatic fashion. "Two chefs with no business sense. What were we thinking?"

"We weren't thinking. We were dreaming." And what was wrong with that?

Nothing. The world was built on dreams. On stories of how fate had intervened at the right time. Like when she'd met Marco. Their partnership was meant to be.

"Well, that dream is quickly turning into a financial nightmare," he said with his usual focus on the bad stuff.

"All right, Mr. Sunshine. Cheer up. We're going to be a huge success. Trust me," she replied over her shoulder as she went back into the pantry to get more flour.

They were going to need it—along with all the good vibes they could throw at the universe. In fact, she'd double hers, since Marco seemed so down about their slow start. No problem, since she had plenty to spare.

Later that afternoon, Claire's mother Helen dropped by, blowing through the seating area of the bakery. She wore a dress in a vivid green with a faux lambswool coat that meant it was still nippy outside. The woman could wear a paper bag and still appear stylish, a talent Claire hadn't inherited, which worked out well for a baker who wore one outfit most days.

But her mom could pass for forty-five despite being more than a decade beyond that, which boded well for Claire in that department if she'd inherited even a smidgen of those stellar genetics.

"Hello, you two," Helen sang as she approached the counter with a smile that meant she had either sold a house, acquired a house to sell, or—more likely—had chased down a poor unsuspecting guy in his thirties on the off chance he might like to meet her single daughter.

They never did. Thankfully.

"Hi, Helen," Marco said. "Would you like some olive bread?"

"Always."

Claire rested both hands on the counter, which wouldn't fortify her for whatever Helen had up her sleeve. "Hey, Mom."

Her mom was her best friend. Which was why Claire was allowed to recognize that her mother's enthusiasm wasn't just her biggest strength, but also the thing that made her overwhelming sometimes.

Helen pulled bundles of rectangular cloth out of her shopping bag and presented them to Claire as if she'd found gold bullion wrapped in twine on the street.

"Um…I already have napkins," Claire said.

Understatement. What she had was a functioning business that she'd built from the ground up. Not that she didn't appreciate the thought. It was just that the bakery was hers. And Marco's too, which meant he got a say but Helen didn't. And besides, Claire didn't call up Helen's clients and offer to show them houses.

"Not as nice as these," Helen informed her pertly. "They were half price, and it was mandatory that I buy them."

The Rules According to Helen. And now Claire owned napkins, whether she intended to or not. "Okay, we'll use them for the engagement party."

A compromise. One that wouldn't hurt her mother's feelings and wouldn't cause the nice gift to go to waste. It *was* a nice gift. Her mother meant well. She did. She just didn't understand how she came across sometimes. A bit like a designer-clad bull in a china shop.

"Did I tell you that I introduced the happy couple?" Helen said brightly. "I'm quite the matchmaker."

"Yes, you mentioned it," Marco said.

"Several times," Claire added, biting her tongue

against the sarcasm since her mother had gotten them the gig.

"Six couples and counting is a pretty good track record," her mom said.

When her mother started trotting out her credentials for finding Claire a boyfriend, it was time to change the subject. Before Helen got to the part where she interfered in her daughter's dating life yet again.

"What time will Tom and Jill be arriving?" Claire asked smoothly.

"Oh, I told everyone to get here at six," Helen said.

Good. Her mom hadn't even blinked at the segue. Claire had been handling her mother for a long time. Long enough to do it effortlessly.

"Well, I…" Marco said, and then circled his finger in Claire's direction to include her. "*We* would like to thank you for having the party here. We certainly could use the business."

"Best food in town. Where else would I have it?" her mother asked lightly.

That's where her mother's blind enthusiasm came in handy, and Claire definitely appreciated it.

"Okay, umm, Marco, will you do decorations?" Claire asked as she glanced at the time. "I have to get home and get ready."

"What are you wearing?" Helen asked with innocence that Claire knew good and well was feigned.

Walked into that one. Her mother lived to advise, especially on fashion. She should've said she was going home to make lemonade or something. "Um, I don't know, the blue wrap dress from Hadley's?"

"Not the low-cut red?" her mother suggested hopefully.

No. Definitely not. "It's a party, Mom, not a date."

"Well, you never know who you might meet."

Yeah. She did. Yet more men who had little patience for a significant other who worked eighty hours a week. Oh, it was okay if *they* did it. But not Claire. Learned that one the hard way.

Besides, she'd yet to meet a man who held a candle to her father or equaled him in romantic gestures that would sweep a woman off her feet, so extending an effort to look nice with such low chances of payoff felt hollow.

Marco, bless him, seemed to clue in on the slight tension that might be pulling at Claire's mouth, because he turned to Helen and said, "Well, I'm going to wear the usual ensemble. What do you think?"

Helen smiled at that, but added to Claire, "You look really good in red."

Not listening, Claire said. In her head, anyway. She'd never utter a word aloud about her mother's taste—it was impeccable. And Helen meant well. She was just boy-crazy, as in crazy over the idea of marrying Claire off to some faceless male. One of these days, Claire would have to figure a way to get through to the woman.

Claire was already in a very serious relationship—with her career. Helen would have to deal with it.

As she headed toward the kitchen to ditch her

apron, Helen leaned over the counter and asked Marco, "Am I too pushy with her?"

Nice, Mom. What, did her mother have no boundaries? Marco was Claire's partner, not an ally in the Find Claire a Husband Campaign.

"Yes," Marco told Helen decisively. "But you wear it very well."

Two

T HE BLUE WRAP DRESS WAS fine. At least, it had
always been fine in the past. Now that Claire
had it on, it felt…frumpy.

Did it *look* frumpy? Claire heaved off the bed and
checked her reflection in the mirror as she slid an earring into each ear. The dress did have a certain elderly-
matron-on-her-way-to-Sunday-brunch vibe about it.
Great. Why hadn't she noticed that before?

Because she'd never had the Helen Michaels'
Outfit Advice soundtrack in her head while wearing
it.

Ugh. Claire wiggled out of the blue dress and into
the low-cut red one. For comparison's sake. Not because she was going to wear it.

Or maybe she was. Who was that woman in the
mirror? Geez. The dress did look ten times better on
her. The mirror hadn't lied about the blue dress; it
wasn't lying now. She might turn a head or two in this
dress. How did her mother *do* that?

Her mother might've won this battle, but definitely not the war.

The red dress meant different shoes, though. She pulled the beige pumps from the back of her closet and buckled them onto her feet, pretty sure she'd be sorry for the additional inches by the end of the night. *Beauty is pain*, she reminded herself, and almost changed back into the blue dress right that instant. What kind of stupid mantra required you to be both beautiful and in pain?

And for what? A man? Not worth it. Instead, she'd wear this dress because she liked it.

No more angsting over an outfit to cater a party. It was dumb to even be thinking about her clothes. She'd be working, not mingling. But at least she'd look good doing it.

As she crossed her condo to fetch her bag, the answering machine clicked on. The machine was old-fashioned, but it still worked, so she hadn't seen a reason to get rid of it. A disembodied male voice floated from it.

"Hi, Claire. You don't know me, but your mother suggested I give you a call."

"Seriously?" she said to the machine and made a face at it.

Claire didn't bother to pick up the phone. Any guy who'd take her mother up on her matchmaking schemes did not deserve a second of Claire's attention.

The disembodied voice continued. "Maybe we could grab dinner tomorrow night? My name is Peter Bloom. Call me back, let me know."

"No." Not just no. *Never.*

"My number is 256—"

Claire grabbed her jacket and slammed the door of her condo for good measure, right as the answering machine clicked off.

When she got to the bakery, she buzzed straight past all of Marco's stellar decorations and cornered her mother in the kitchen.

"Who is Peter Bloom?"

At least Helen had the grace to look slightly chagrined, but definitely not chagrined enough for the crime in question, at least not as far as Claire was concerned.

"Peter, yes." Her mother smoothed her hair self-consciously. "He came to an open house of mine. He didn't end up buying. But a single man shopping for a four-bedroom? I guess he wants to start a family."

Claire rolled her eyes, because really? Maybe he wanted to start a hotel for dogs. Unless he'd expressly told her mother that he was looking for a wife to go along with his house, Helen needed to butt out.

"Mom, you have to stop setting me up."

Especially with men Claire had never met. Or men she had met. Men she'd dated a few times and had lost interest in. All of them were off limits.

Claire wheeled toward the sink to dump the plate she'd snagged as her excuse for being in the kitchen, instead of out front ensuring everything was running smoothly. Which was where she should be instead of back here telling her mom yet again to lay off.

Helen followed her to the sink, still making excuses for her overbearing behavior. Still fussing over Claire with maternal concern practically dripping from her expression. Her mom reached out to adjust the neckline of Claire's dress.

"Oh, Claire, pretty soon your dad and I are going be off traveling the globe, and if he has his way, we are not going to be home much. I hate the idea of you being alone."

"I'm not alone! I am here, at the bakery, twenty-four/seven, which is exactly where I want to be. There's plenty of time for me to find someone and fall in love."

It wasn't that Claire hated the idea of meeting someone. It was just... Well, she wanted to meet someone. Like, literally *meet* them, in a special, fate-filled way that would clue her in instantly that she'd met The One.

Meanwhile, she had a bakery to run until those stars aligned.

"There is nothing wrong with building your business, but you can't plan when you're going to fall in love," Helen insisted.

Says the woman who was doing everything in her power to stack the deck toward that exact outcome. "Look. I love this place. It is enough for me. It's more than enough, believe me, okay?"

"Hey," her dad said as he came into the kitchen, looking dapper in casual dress instead of the three-piece suit he'd worn for so many years to his job as a financial consultant. "Don't you look beautiful."

Saved by the well-placed compliment. "Thank you, Dad."

Sam kissed both of her cheeks in turn, then focused

on Helen. "Marco says that there is a wine festival in Florence that we would love. Not a bad way to launch our retirement."

"Sounds nice," Claire said brightly.

Helen made a face. "I am not ready for retirement. I'm still in my prime. Okay, late prime, maybe, but that's as much as I'll concede."

"Please go mingle," Claire told her parents, pointing to the seating area in question. Which wasn't her kitchen. "I have it all from here."

"We've been dismissed," Helen murmured to Sam and let him escort her out of Claire's domain.

The engagement party went extremely well, especially for the first of such events Claire and Marco had both catered and hosted. The whole thing had turned out nice, thanks to Marco's bang-up touch with centerpieces. Claire had half expected it to be difficult to play both guest and official food provider, but that hadn't been the case at all.

Claire's uncle meandered to the head of the long table full of Michaels' relatives wearing his "time for a toast" face and carrying a flute half full of champagne. Arnie dinged the side of the glass with a spoon to get everyone's attention, then cleared his throat.

"I'd like to thank all of you for coming, and I'd like to raise a glass to Jill and…" Arnie paused and glanced at his daughter's fiancé with feigned confusion, as if he'd forgotten the guy's name. Everyone tittered with appreciation at the joke. "Tom? Tom. A lifetime of love and happiness."

With the last words, Arnie got serious, and his voice reflected the affection and emotion of the moment. His little girl was getting married—a bitter-sweet rite of passage Claire could tell he hadn't quite prepared for.

"Cheers," the crowd called out and clinked glasses of champagne with those sitting around them.

Claire was so moved by the sentiment that she couldn't help but share a warm smile with her mother, who was sitting next to her. They'd gone a whole hour or so without Helen mentioning a word about setting up Claire with one of the groomsmen. A record. But appreciated. This evening was about Jill and Tom. And the amazing coconut lime tarts that everyone had devoured. Not one remained.

Jill floated to the head of the table to join her dad, and it was clear she had her own toast in mind.

"And I would like to toast my aunt, Helen, for introducing me and Tom. We can't thank you enough."

Ugh. Claire glanced down at her plate, scared her eyeroll had been loud enough for everyone to hear. Not that she begrudged her cousin's happiness or Jill's right to thank the one responsible for the matchmaking. It was just that Helen added such accolades to her resume, and would trot out the success at some indeterminate point in the future when she needed to remind Claire that Jill had ended up married and happy because she'd respected her Aunt Helen's taste in men.

"I couldn't be happier for you two," Helen said, but Claire knew what she meant was, *I'd like to be saying the same thing at Claire's engagement party.*

"Cheers," Jill said, followed by repeat calls around the room.

"All right," Arnie said. "Drinks are on my big brother over at the bar. Let's go!"

Helen leaned in to be extra sure Claire heard her. "I'm glad someone appreciates my advice."

"Of course she does," Claire allowed with a stiff smile. "Because you haven't been advising her since birth. What to eat, what to wear, who to date."

"Oh, Claire, so dramatic. You know sometimes it takes someone with perspective to—"

"Mom, please stop. Stop intervening. I am perfectly happy as I am."

"Okay." Helen threw up her hands in surrender. "I get it, loud and clear."

Not likely. But it would do for tonight, and there was no point in rehashing this old argument yet again. This evening was about family and celebrating Jill and Tom. "Good, now go have some fun."

Helen vanished into the crowd as the music swelled and relatives took to the makeshift dance floor, which Marco had created by moving several tables over against the far wall. It was a good reminder that the bakery could be multipurpose in the future for other types of events.

Marco crossed the room and sat down in Helen's empty spot. It was the first chance Claire had gotten to speak to him since the evening had begun. But instead of making a comment about money, or lack thereof, he smiled, his gaze on the clean-cut guy in his late twenties who was currently chatting with Helen.

"Let's face it. Sometimes we all just need someone to dance with."

Even Marco was in on the joke. He knew her

mother was out of control. Why couldn't Helen see that her meddling was affecting the close relationship they'd always shared as mother and daughter?

"Do you want to dance?" Claire asked him, because at this point, that sounded far better than whatever Helen had in mind to do with Clean-Cut Boy.

"Hey, cuz," Jill said brightly as she slid into the seat on the other side of Claire and took her hand. "So, one of Tom's friends wants to meet you."

Oh, clever. This was the first time Helen had sent an envoy in her stead. If the message came from Jill, the happy bride, surely Claire wouldn't see through that, right?

All at once, Claire wasn't in a charitable mood. "The one standing next to my mom."

It wasn't a question, and Jill didn't bother to pretend she misunderstood. "Busted."

"Yeah." Claire shook her head once and murmured to Marco. "That is my cue to leave."

Claire gathered dishes in her wake as she breezed back to the kitchen, thanking the extra wait staff as she passed them. They'd done a phenomenal job in her stead as she played the part of a guest. The expense had cut into the bottom line, but it had been worth it to pull off a great event.

Why couldn't Helen see that Claire loved her job, loved being good at desserts, and didn't need help running her life?

And her mother picked that inopportune moment to follow Claire into the kitchen.

The note of exasperation slipped out. "What part of *I'm perfectly happy as I am* do you not understand?"

Helen smiled. "I was just going to say the tart was terrific."

Right when Claire thought her mother had taken things too far, she went and did something unexpected like that. The compliment went a long way toward smoothing things over and she laughed softly.

"That is my favorite thing in the world," Helen said softly.

"What?"

"My daughter's smile."

They shared a moment of solidarity, throwing Claire back to an earlier time when they'd both been on the same page. Back when she'd first gone to culinary school and it had seemed as if her mother really understood what drove Claire—baking. Creating. Giving people little bits of sunshine they could hold in their hands and then eat; it was the best way to spread love that Claire knew.

"So," Helen said cheerily. "Peter Bloom?"

But she followed it with a wink that somehow took the sting out of it. Maybe Helen was in on the joke, too.

"You are relentless," Claire told her, still smiling.

Her mother loved her and wanted to help. Claire got that. She'd just have to keep dealing with the way her mother showed that love and go on. After all, Helen had introduced Jill to Tom. Maybe it wouldn't kill Claire to go out with Peter. But she'd offer to pay.

Three

THE RESTAURANT PETER BLOOM HAD picked had passable tablecloths, great champagne, and an unfortunate view of the bore her mother had set her up with.

Honestly, the man talked nonstop. About his job, mostly, unless he happened to veer off on a different subject, like his hobbies. That only lasted for a few moments, and then they landed right back into the courtroom, where Peter—as he'd told her over and over—was the best trial lawyer in existence, apparently.

"I'm standing there in the middle of the courtroom, all eyes on me, and suddenly it occurs to me—" He paused for one second to pick up the bottle of bubbly from the bucket of ice. "Do you want some more champagne?"

"No." That would make this date last longer.

Peter didn't even hear her, just poured more into her glass without even noticing her wince.

"I have a whole lot to celebrate," he told her. Again. "Anyways, it occurs to me that what I have is not just a point of law, but an actual breach of contract. Needless to say, I won the case."

He accompanied this astounding proclamation by flashing both hands, fingers spread, as if he'd dropped bombs.

He'd dropped something, all right. Claire's interest.

"Wow," she commented. Needlessly. Peter was already off and running at the mouth again.

"My goal is to have my own firm by the time I'm forty."

No doubt he would, but Claire had no intention of being around to see it. Or frankly, even the next hour of Peter Bloom's life. "Unfortunately, Peter, my goal is to go to sleep. I'm sorry. I've just been up since dawn."

"Yeah, sure," Peter said.

Clearly, he hadn't clued in yet that this date was a disaster, and Claire didn't have the energy to explain why.

In a great big ha-ha from the universe, it was drizzling when Claire exited the restaurant. Fitting. She opened the spare umbrella she kept in her purse and dashed to her car, glad she'd at least scored a parking place not too far from the door. Peter had valeted, naturally.

As she fought bumper-to-bumper traffic, she called her mom through the integrated phone feature of her car that allowed her to verbally dial.

Helen's voice reverberated through the speakers. "Claire, I'm so glad you called! How was it?"

"Ugh, Mom. It was awful. Clearly this is not one of your more inspired matches."

"No one bats a thousand."

It sounded like Helen might be in the kitchen or bathroom, judging by the way she echoed and what could be running water in the background.

"He returned his entree *twice*, and he couldn't stop talking about himself at the top of his lungs."

Claire rolled to a stop at a red light and glanced out the window. A man jogged by in a distinctive blue rainproof jacket. He seemed…familiar. As if she'd noticed him jogging before, maybe, or perhaps he'd come into the bakery. Hard to place him, though. He was wearing a knit ski hat in deference to the weather, a necessary evil in a place that rained so often.

"Next time I'll be more careful," Helen told her. "The vetting will be exhaustive."

"No, no. There's not going to be a next time. That is the last straw. Please. I will know when the right guy comes along. You've got to promise me—no more." Helen didn't say anything in the pause. "Mom, do you hear me?"

The man in blue stopped to pet a dog being walked by a lady with an umbrella. Wouldn't it be nice to meet a guy while out for a walk, totally by chance?

The romance of the idea nearly took her breath away. That was what she wanted. Something completely random that turned into an event of significance she could tell her kids and grandkids about later. A crossing of paths cloaked in fate with a side of destiny. She'd meet the gaze of her future love and *know* it was meant to be.

Like the way it had happened for her own mom and dad. They'd fallen for each other instantly over the last copy of *A Room with a View* at their college bookstore. Of all people, Helen should understand that Claire wanted something special instead of a contrived bait-and-hook approach to finding love.

If it happened like that, she might make room in her life for a man. The bakery was demanding, but she could envision carving out time for the right person. Meaning someone *not* handed to her by her mother.

The jogger moved out of her line of sight, dragging her attention back to the fruitless conversation with her mother.

"Whatever you say," Helen said. "Good night, dear."

The light turned green, and Claire hit the gas pedal. "Good night, Mom."

Helen pressed the end call button on her phone well before she'd been ready to end the call. That was the way everything seemed to go as of late—over before she'd barely blinked. Claire's childhood and her precocious teen years had vanished in a blur, and here they were, about to say goodbye to her daughter's twenties.

It was a travesty that you couldn't stop time. Especially when Sam and Claire didn't seem overly bothered by how it was slipping away. Both of them.

Clueless. All they had to do was look at Helen's face, and they'd see what the years did to a woman.

Helen poked at the wrinkles that she'd claim were laugh lines if anyone asked. They certainly weren't funny. How was it possible to age on the outside but still feel like you hadn't quite figured out how to be a grownup? Oh, sure, women begged her for her secret to looking young all the time, but the point wasn't whether she could lie about her birthday and get away with it. Her face had still become this gauge of time that she couldn't change, and it was maddening.

She wandered into the bedroom, where Sam had already taken up residence on his side of the bed, his cute reading glasses perched on his nose as he wrote notes in his journal.

"You have to let her find love on her own time, on her own terms," he said mildly.

He'd been listening to her part of the conversation, obviously, and, as always, had already taken Claire's side.

"Hopefully in my lifetime," Helen countered and shut the door of the closet, where she'd carefully hung the ironed outfit she'd wear tomorrow for the Brewer showing.

Mrs. Brewer had rejected the first couple of houses Helen had shown her. Mr. Brewer only cared about the garage. As long as he had room for his 1967 Corvette, the rest of the house could be full of faux wood paneling and ugly floral carpet for all he cared.

Which meant Helen needed to look like a woman who knew her kitchens and bathrooms, the things that were important to Mrs. Brewer. A Hilltop Street house in Bellevue had come on the market, and she had a feeling about it...

She could match houses to people just as well as she could match people to people. If only Claire would stop being so stubborn and let her help, she'd find the right man for her daughter. With all the negative vibes Claire was putting out there, no wonder none of the matches had worked out.

"I think she's still hurt that it didn't work out last time," Sam said.

Not that old argument again. It was silly to let one relationship failure dictate the future possibilities. "She can't dwell on the past. She needs to move on."

"Maybe you're the one that needs to move on, honey. We need to book those tickets."

Ah, and here we are with the new argument. The one for retirement. Might as well call it deadment.

"We'll get to it," she said noncommittally as she climbed into her side of the bed and squeezed lotion on her hand.

They were so dry lately. Another fun symptom of getting older. The humidity could be in ninety-percent range, and yet her skin felt like Egyptian papyrus that had been discovered in a two-thousand-year-old pyramid.

"What's the reluctance? We've been planning this new chapter of our lives for years. Our grand Italian adventure."

That was the question she'd dreaded him asking. But now that he had, she needed him to understand that she wasn't completely on board with his plans. Or rather, the idea of the plans didn't bother her, but it would be much better if they were future plans instead of right-now plans.

"I like this chapter. I'm not ready to move on."

"But we get the best of both. Half a year traveling, half a year at home," he said in his pragmatic fashion that had served him well in his role as a financial advisor for so many years.

"I guess."

"Stop guessing, and just do this with me."

Ugh, he was not letting this go. "I want to, Sam. I really do. It's just… Retirement."

"Don't think of it as retirement. Think of it as a six-month vacation."

That was so easy for him to say. He'd said *sayonara* to his clients with remarkable ease. Some of them he'd been working with for years, had guided them into their own retirement while planning his. He'd been thinking about this stage far longer than she had. Somehow she'd convinced herself if she ignored the march of time, this day would never come.

Funny how that hadn't worked.

"Well, it's a marker though," she told him. One that couldn't be reversed. Once she said *okay*, she couldn't take it back. "Another name for getting old. You know, I keep thinking I'm twenty-three."

"So. Be twenty-three in Italy. If you want to stay busy with work the other six months, then you have that option."

"Right."

And the real twenty-three-year-olds had more energy, better tools for finding new clients, and would eat her lunch if she took a sabbatical. This was the worst season to be out of the game. That option didn't work for her, not now. Not for the foreseeable future.

"We still have a lot of time ahead of us. If you keep feeding me kale, sheesh, we could live forever."

Well, yeah. So what was the hurry?

He stuck his reading glasses back on as she held out her hand for him to take, which he did. Because they were a team. Always had been, always would be. That was what love looked like in their world, and her heart still warmed when she looked at him, even after all these years.

He'd aged so gracefully, his hair turning silver almost without her noticing. It didn't detract from his appearance an iota. In some ways, he was more handsome now than he'd been in college. She certainly could say their shared history created a bond that meant more than physical appearances in any event.

"It's a deal," she said. Being immortal had a certain appeal, after all. "Just understand that I need a little time to take it all in."

"Okay."

His voice rang with sincerity. He meant it. She'd explained that he was moving too fast for her, and he'd understood.

"Thanks."

It was a good thing they'd talked. Why had she dreaded this conversation so much? Because she hadn't wanted to disappoint him, that was why. He'd been talking about this trip for years.

But he was still the same guy she'd been married to for decades, and he cared about her. Of course Sam had been reasonable about waiting on the tickets. She'd worried needlessly about telling him she wanted to wait.

Italy would still be there in six months.

But in the morning, Sam followed his usual routine of mentioning little tidbits he'd learned about Italy during his travel research, almost as if the conversation the night before hadn't happened. While he cared about her and her needs, he had his own agenda that might not be as easily swayed as she might've hoped.

She had to get away from all the Italy talk. Just for a few hours so she could get her head on straight.

Helen called Claire to see if she wanted to go shopping after the Brewer showing, something they hadn't done together in a while because the bakery took up so much of her daughter's time. And things had been…strained lately between them. They'd always been so close, and then out of nowhere, Claire had started pushing back, getting downright testy about Helen's perfectly innocent help in the boyfriend area.

Goodness, it wasn't like Claire was doing anything about it on her own. You'd think she'd welcome a date handed to her on a silver platter. Well, one who wasn't a bore anyway.

Miraculously, Claire said yes to shopping. So she wasn't too mad about Peter Bloom.

He hadn't been right for her. She could see that now. He'd been looking for a house so he could entertain, and she'd mistakenly thought that meant entertaining alongside a wife who'd be his equal, a woman with a great personality, not a timid, fade-into-the-background type who'd be okay with someone who hogged all the limelight.

Next time, she'd ask a few more questions before slipping Claire's name into the conversation.

The department store wasn't all that crowded, a rarity for a Sunday. She and Claire were able to chat as they dug through the half-off jewelry table.

"If I keep whining about Italy, your father is going to go alone, and I wouldn't blame him."

"What're you so afraid of?" Claire asked.

A legitimate question, the one she should've been asking herself. What Sam had called reluctance, her daughter had rightly labeled fear.

She was afraid. Of so many things. Not just getting old and becoming irrelevant, but of Claire not finding someone to build a life with. She didn't seem to understand that adulthood passed by in a blur, and then *bam*. Your husband starts talking about retirement right when it felt like you were finally getting settled into your professional niche.

She rubbed at the place in her chest that had gone tight as she thought about actually giving her up her entire career. And what the man she loved would say if she told him she couldn't do it. That even six months was too long in the dog-eat-dog real estate profession.

"I don't know," Helen admitted as she tried to answer Claire's question honestly. "Losing my daily routine, being away from you. I mean, who am I if I'm not your mother? I have a very precarious sense of myself. I'm nuts, right?"

A joke was the best way to turn the conversation away from the raw truth Claire had unwittingly helped reveal.

"You're just figuring that out now?" Claire teased gently.

A flash of pink caught Helen's eye, and she pulled a floral skirt from the rack in front of her, holding it up to the top Claire had been carrying around for the last ten minutes. "Oh, look at this. This one on the clearance rack missing the skirt, and this discounted beauty missing a top."

Claire's gaze swept over the ensemble. "Wow, you do have a good eye."

"I do where you're concerned." Now, if she'd let her mother take care of all of the missing pieces in her life, Claire would be much happier. "You see, if I was in Italy, that top and that bottom never would have met."

"That is true."

Even Claire could see the wisdom of waiting on Italy. If only Helen could convince Sam of the same, everything would be golden.

Claire darted over to the full-length mirror and held up the outfit with a critical eye as Helen crossed to stand behind her. The pink was gorgeous and suited Claire's complexion to a T.

"Ooh, something to wear on your next blind date?" Helen commented lightly.

"That's not funny."

No, because it hadn't been a joke. The sense of time slipping through the hourglass wouldn't abate. If Helen was going to find someone for Claire, she had to do it now. Before Sam dragged Helen all the way to Italy, where she wouldn't have the ability to take an impromptu shopping trip with her daughter when the mood struck.

She couldn't put off Sam's dreams forever.

Four

AFTER THE PLEASANT SHOPPING TRIP with her mother, Claire went home and had a quiet dinner alone.

Her mother had been so preoccupied while they'd been together. Retirement was really weighing on her, much more so than Helen had let on. Claire could tell. She and her mom had always been close, but once Claire had reached adulthood, they'd become fast friends, conferring with each other about everything from dreams to career challenges to shoes.

Until her mother's matchmaking fever had taken hold, afflicting their relationship worse than a bout of malaria.

Hopefully, they were moving past all of that. With as many times as Claire had lain down the law, Helen should be an expert in the matter of Claire v. Forced Blind Dates.

Once she'd changed into her PJ's, Claire couldn't resist the lure of her laptop. She'd had her eye on this beauty of a convection oven that was way out of her price range. But it was free to dream.

She sat at the desk, setting aside her cup of chamomile tea, a staple she never ran out of during the rainy season. The webpage with all of the ovens was already open in her browser. Basically, she never closed it. The shiny new ovens marching across the product pages formed a sort of goal board. If goals could actually be called that when they were completely out of reach.

If she stared at them hard enough, eventually one would materialize in her bakery, right?

An even better oven than the one she'd had her eye on popped up in the ribbon showing what people eventually bought after viewing the current item.

She clicked on it, and when the bigger view spilled onto her screen, she glanced through the product specifications. Wow. Everything she needed and then some.

"That's a good one," she murmured to her screen.

Couldn't hurt to put out the right vibes into the universe. Sometimes fate worked like that. You wished for something hard enough, and it started the gears in motion that led to something great coming together later on.

The ad space next to the specs shifted from a furniture store to a pink-and-purple splash ad for Destiny Match. That one had been coming up a lot lately for some reason, and it was the kind of vibe she didn't need.

Dating sites did not work. She hated them. That was how she'd met her ex-boyfriend Ron the Jerk, as she'd dubbed him, because that was the politest name she could use in mixed company. He was at least ninety percent of the reason she believed love couldn't be forced down anyone's throat—it had to happen organically. Magically. That was the kind of love that lasted, when you met someone by chance because all the stars aligned. You had fate on your side from moment one.

Weird, though, that she was still getting ads for dating sites when it had been over a year since she'd visited one. The company must not have a clue how to target their ads to go to current members only. Their loss. Claire would never click on something like that.

Not when she had the bakery to focus on.

Helen couldn't sleep. Guilty conscience. Claire would kill her if she found out Helen had created a profile in her daughter's name on a dating site.

Worse, Helen had started chatting with matches while pretending to be Claire.

It had seemed like a good idea at the time. What better way to find someone who'd be compatible with Claire than a dating site? There were tons of people who met the loves of their lives online every day. Helen had even shown a house to a newly engaged couple the other day who had mentioned Destiny Match as the dating site where they'd found each other.

But after Claire had been so adamant about Helen not fixing her up anymore, she just…couldn't keep up this ruse.

Careful not to disturb Sam, Helen slipped out from under the covers and padded into the study, where she turned on her computer so she could log into Claire's profile on Destiny Match.

Okay, it was Helen's profile. Not Claire's. But she'd used Claire's stats and a lovely picture of her at Green Lake Park.

A message popped up from David, a man Destiney Match had picked for Claire.

I'm looking forward to meeting you on Thursday.

He was super cute, a lawyer…like Peter Bloom. Obviously, that wasn't going to work. She'd have to go in and specify no lawyers in Claire's profile.

No, no. She was deleting the profile and erasing all traces of her "meddling," as Claire called it, and her daughter would be none the wiser.

Helen popped open the message box and started typing.

I'm afraid I have to

She took her fingers off the keyboard before she could type the last word, *cancel.* David was a great guy, funny, not too full of himself. At least online, anyway. In person, he could be horrible, but she didn't think he'd be *that* different from his picture and stats.

Okay, well sure, he could be. Kind of like Claire would be completely different from her online persona, given that she hadn't been the one chatting with David in the first place.

But…

Claire wasn't getting this done on her own. And who knew Claire better than her own mother? No one. She'd nailed Claire's voice easily, so it was practically like David *had* been chatting with the woman in the profile picture. Helen backspaced and retyped.

Me too.

It was done. Claire was meeting David on Thursday. Now Helen had to figure out how to make that happen.

The Farmer's Market was one of Claire's favorite places. The local vendors had started recognizing her and Marco, and thanks to some well-placed compliments on the produce offered, some had started saving back the best stuff for them.

The tomatoes they'd scored would rock in the tomato basil soup she'd added to the menu. Fresh cream would be a must. Better quality than what she'd been buying. They might have to spring for the delivery service that catered to the downtown restaurants, which Marco had balked at thus far. But he'd come around.

Her phone vibrated in her pocket. Claire pulled it out and read the message. Her pulse spiked. Wow, when her mother came through, she really came through.

"Hey," she called to Marco as they exited the market at the east end on Minor Avenue. "My mom just texted me. She got us a gig. Catering a fundraiser at an art gallery."

It was a peace offering and apology wrapped up in

one. Her mother felt bad about setting Claire up with Peter and wanted to make it up to her. She'd take a nice paycheck in exchange all day long.

"Wow, she may be driving you crazy, but she is definitely good for business," Marco said and shifted their haul to his other hand.

He always insisted on carrying the bags, a throwback to the manners his Italian mother had impressed on him growing up. Claire didn't mind letting him be chivalrous, especially since it wasn't raining, which made their walk back to the bakery nice instead of something to endure.

The rhythm of Seattle drifted through her: the hum of car tires on asphalt, the slap of people's feet as they strolled past, the far distant bleat of horns from ships passing through Puget Sound.

There wasn't another place on earth as harmonious.

"Easy for you to say," she told him. "she's not micromanaging your life. Maybe we can use this opportunity to pass out coupons for the bakery."

It was an idea she'd been toying with but hadn't had the chance to bring up yet. An influx of cash in the form of a new catering event made it the perfect time.

Marco wasn't so keen on the idea, judging by his expression. "Great, so now we're gonna work for free."

No, not even close. It made total sense in her mind, but when you had a warm audience in your hand, you didn't skip out before giving them a reason to come check out the bakery that had all the same food they'd enjoyed at the art gallery event.

"No, on the contrary, this gig actually affords us a new oven."

That seemed to be enough to get Marco's attention. He paused at the corner of Minor and Lynn, where the clatter of boats at the Lake Union marina were the loudest. The overcast sky threatened to change the speed of their walk at any minute.

"Okay listen. I know that this is a long shot, but I know a guy who knows a guy who knows a guy who could contact that online restaurant critic The Wandering Gourmet. Maybe we could get him to come out."

That was the spirit. All of her positive vibes were finally starting to take a hold of her partner. Engaging The Wandering Gourmet was a fantastic idea, one that got her so excited she could hardly contain herself. The restaurant critic had quite a following in Seattle, enough that it could put them on the map.

She exhaled with measured cadence. "A positive review from him—"

"Would be like winning the lottery, I know. Which is almost impossible."

Okay, that was the Marco she was used to, more doom and gloom than sunshine. But that was why they were a good match. She had more than enough positive vibes to share.

"Have a little faith," she said.

"On a lighter note, the gas bill is overdue."

For whatever reason, that made her smile in spite of it all. "Great."

They were going to turn a corner soon. She could feel it. This new catering gig would be the start of something amazing, and then she could tell Marco, *I told you so.*

And that was why she didn't have time for her mother's shenanigans. The bakery was her first love. If by random chance she met someone, fine. Otherwise, she had an art gallery fundraiser to keep her very happy. With any luck, they could have a new oven by the middle of the month.

A man who could only be David wandered into the bar, clearly looking for Claire. His gaze slid right over Helen, which was a good sign, but it definitely didn't help her feel any younger, that was for sure.

He was really cute, too, clean-cut and not wearing a suit. He'd be perfect for Claire if she could somehow convince him that Claire not being here in person wasn't weird, and that if he'd just get over the unorthodox method, there was nothing wrong with meeting a woman through her mother.

"David," she called brightly.

A confused expression stole over his face. "Can I help you?"

"My name is Helen Michaels. I'm actually Claire's mother."

She flashed the profile picture on her phone as if

that was in and of itself a credential. Hopefully he had a sense of humor.

"Did something happen? Is she okay?"

Oh, his concern was a good sign. Only someone with the right character would care about the well-being of someone he'd yet to meet.

"No, nothing happened. She's not even here." Helen punctuated that with a laugh she prayed didn't sound as forced to him as it did to her. "She doesn't even know about us meeting. You're going to find this hilarious, but I made that profile on Destiny Match myself. I was just trying to help her find a boyfriend. Can we sit?"

He sat. So far so good. As long as he didn't run screaming from the building, she might pull this off.

She cleared her throat. "Let me just start by saying I know how strange this all must seem to you."

David gave a laugh that sounded self-conscious. But it was still a laugh. She'd bank on him having that sense of humor she'd detected.

"That would be an understatement," he said.

"Uh-huh. The truth is, I'm not even supposed to be doing this. My daughter—Claire—if she knew I was doing this again—"

"Wait, you've done this before?"

Bad choice of words. David was looking decidedly less enthusiastic about this whole endeavor, which wasn't saying much, since he hadn't been jumping for joy in the first place.

You're blowing it. It was on her to sell Claire's wonderful attributes, and she really needed to close the deal.

"Well, only a few times, and it didn't really work out. Mostly with sons of friends, relatives of friends, you know…the usual. Oh, and don't worry, this actually was her picture on the profile."

She picked up her phone to point to Claire's picture again, solely to remind David that she was still representing the real woman she'd pretended to be.

"Excuse me, I just need to ask you: why are you telling me this?"

A legitimate question, one she should've had an answer to already. "Oh… Well, I suppose because I wanted you to—"

"You know what? I'm just going to cut my losses and get out of here."

David stood, settling his lightweight jacket onto his arm.

Mayday! Damage control time.

"Oh no, wait. No," she called.

"It was nice meeting you, and good luck finding your daughter a date. You're going to need it."

He turned to walk away, and Helen couldn't help one last-ditch effort to keep him from leaving. "Look, everything I wrote about her was true."

But he was already at the end of the bar. He called back over his shoulder, "You left out the part about her crazy mother."

Well, that stung.

Worse, David's exodus had attracted the attention

of the guy sitting at the end of the bar, who'd apparently heard every word of the exchange and found the whole thing terribly amusing.

Five

THE CRAZY LADY WHO'D SET up a fake profile for her daughter, and then had actually met a man at a bar on her daughter's behalf, sank back down onto the bar stool with such a defeated air about her that Eric couldn't help but notice.

His heart kind of went out to her. She was definitely a little off-center, but sometimes parents did whacked-out things on behalf of their children. Granted, the ones who came into his medical practice were usually looking for a way to stop their kids from suffering through the symptoms of the flu or something to ease the pain of a broken arm.

But still. He'd become a pediatrician because he liked helping kids. He and the parents were on the same side.

"House Chardonnay, please," she said to the bartender.

"Having a rough night?" he asked her with genuine concern.

He shouldn't encourage her. But Dana was late—totally understandable, as she had a demanding practice as a surgeon—and he'd been sitting here with nothing to do but watch the free entertainment in the form of this lady.

And she had this look about her, as if she needed a friend. It wouldn't sit well on his conscience to ignore her.

"You heard all that, huh?" she asked.

He would've had to have been deaf not to. And besides, this scenario was far too intriguing to pretend otherwise. "Sorry, it's a quiet bar."

"Can anyone actually die from embarrassment?" she asked with far more self-awareness than he'd have credited.

Apparently, she did have a sense of when she'd gone completely overboard. Some parents didn't. But this whole scene shouldn't have happened in the first place then. Maybe there was more to the story than first appeared.

"So, let me get this straight. You were posing as your daughter on a dating site?"

"Yeah."

Or not. Sounded pretty much like straight-up bonkers to him.

"Yeah, I'd be mortified if I was her. I mean, I'm sure your heart was in the right place," he amended quickly as the lady's face fell.

"The heart has a mind of its own."

And sometimes the heart knew exactly what it was doing and did it anyway, even when all of the signs pointed out where you were going wrong. "Do you mind if I ask what prompted this strange behavior?"

43

The lady deflated a bit more. "I have no idea what made me do it. I mean, why did I even come here tonight? I promised my daughter I would back off. If she found out, she would disown me."

Okay, so she really did seem pretty harmless. Misguided, sure. But his own mom had certainly pushed women in his direction often enough that he recognized the sentiment. Moms wanted their children to be happy. On top of that, they wanted grand-kids, and they weren't above a little maneuvering to get them. Kids were great. He wanted a few himself someday. Not on demand, of course. But in due time.

"Well, for what it's worth, my lips are sealed." Eric mimed locking his lips with two fingers. "She's very pretty, by the way."

"I'm sorry?"

He pointed at the lady's phone. "Oh, your daughter. I saw a picture of her earlier when you were showing the other guy."

"Oh, yeah. You're very sweet." The lady slid from her seat and crossed over to hold out her hand. "I'm Helen, by the way."

"Eric Carlton."

"So what do you do, Eric?" Helen asked as she settled back onto her bar stool, chardonnay in hand.

"I'm a pediatrician."

"Are you married?"

And this started sounding like a fishing trip of the sort that needed to be nipped in the bud immediately.

"No, Helen, I am not. In fact, I'm waiting for someone. There she is."

Dana stormed into the bar in what might be the best case of excellent timing she'd ever had. Except her face had this frazzled edge to it—not the look of a woman who was looking forward to a date.

"Hi," he called to her.

"Hi, Eric. Sorry I'm late. It's been one of those days. Did you get a table?" she asked, but it was clear from the vague expression on her pretty face that she was barely there mentally.

"Yes, it'll be ready in a minute."

She draped her coat over the empty chair next to him, her frame vibrating with energy, which was one of the most attractive things about her. "Oh, and before I forget, I can't make that artsy fundraiser thing on Saturday. Something's come up."

Something always came up with Dana. They'd been trying to get this date on the books for two weeks, as it stood. But he couldn't fault her. No doctor got to fully dictate their personal time.

"Okay that's fine, I'll probably just—"

A shrill, insistent ring tone from the depths of Dana's bag interrupted him. That was becoming a startlingly frequent occurrence too.

"I need to get this," she said and dug out her phone. "I have a patient coming out of surgery. Just a sec. This is Doctor Becker."

Dana darted off to the quiet alcove on the far end of the bar, leaving Eric alone. Again. And apparently it had been his turn to provide the free entertainment for Helen this time around.

She smiled sympathetically as she caught his gaze.

"Let me guess, your first date?"

"Second," he corrected, though it should have been their fifth or sixth if you counted all of the canceled ones.

Helen nodded sagely and sipped her Chardonnay. "It won't last."

"Excuse me?" She had a lot of nerve, butting into his new relationship with Dana, like she knew anything about how hard it was to date as a doctor, let alone when you were dating another doctor.

He could be patient. No pun intended.

"I'm a real estate agent," Helen said like that explained anything. "After twenty years of selling houses, I can tell which couples will last. It's the respect, the laughter, the look in the eyes, versus the ones who need me to sell the house when they split up. You and Doctor Gorgeous are not a good match."

Helen waved her hand in Dana's direction, who was still on the phone, pacing back and forth with a worried frown that told Eric the surgery hadn't gone as well as she'd hoped.

"Okay." Not much else to say to that.

Especially when he had the sinking suspicion she might be right.

"Let me give you my card in case you're ever in the market," she said.

Helen handed him a card and left the bar. He glanced at the writing, not that he expected it to say anything other than what it did. *Helen Michaels, Real Estate Agent.* She was exactly as advertised: a mom who sold houses in between bouts of trolling websites for unsuspecting men who might be willing to take her daughter on a date.

A devoted mom who loved her daughter.

Dana ended her call and joined him at the bar. "Who was that woman?"

"Just a real estate agent. Trying to sell me something."

"Well, you would not believe the day that I've had," she said, easily changing the subject to her own troubles as she pushed back her shoulder-length dark hair. "Back-to-back surgeries that lasted hours longer than they should have, thanks to incompetent scheduling."

Eric relaxed into the conversation. Medical speak, he understood. He and Dana were a good match, despite Helen's supposition to the contrary. They had lots in common and had gone to the same medical school, though they'd never met because Eric had been a few years ahead of her.

They'd finally crossed paths through a mutual friend. That was how everyone he knew met their significant other. Why would it work any differently for him?

Helen's warning stuck in his mind as Dana droned on and on about the procedure she'd done earlier on an elderly patient, which he'd normally be fascinated by. There was something off about her tonight, though, a preoccupation with her own experiences that he'd never noticed before.

What was wrong with him? Dana was great. Beautiful. Accomplished. But he couldn't help wondering when she'd notice that she hadn't even asked him about his day yet.

Mornings at the practice Eric shared with his friend Nate were usually the busiest time, but today was extra crazy. So far, Eric had treated a case of pinkeye, a baby with an ear infection, and two cases of poison ivy, one of which the poor kid's mom had insisted was Ebola because she'd read on the internet that it came with a rash. It didn't, and also, there were currently no documented cases of Ebola in Seattle, so it would be practically impossible for the little boy to have the disease.

The internet was the worst place to get medical information, yet so many of his patients' parents researched their children's symptoms online and then came into his office armed with their own diagnosis.

Sometimes he didn't even get a word in edgewise until after the frightened mom or dad had spewed out the entire contents of a medical article that bore no relevance to the matter at hand—getting their kid well.

That was where Dr. Eric came in. And he loved his job, kooky parents and all.

By ten o'clock, he needed a breather and jetted to the front to have Donna take care of some paperwork. As he glanced through the forms attached to his clipboard, he started to call out the instructions, but Donna was talking to someone.

Eric gave her a minute, still preoccupied with the details of the forms and only half listening to the conversation.

"I'm Donna Statton," his receptionist was saying to the person standing in front of her. "You sold me my house. We still live there. Over in Kirkland."

"Well, you just made my day," the lady she was talking to said in response.

Sounded like a wrap-up of the conversation to him, and he needed this insurance paperwork filed as soon as possible due to the elevated risk of denial. That way they could get started on counterclaims. It was a song and dance he hated playing with the insurance companies, but a necessity in his field.

"Donna," he said. "I'm going to need you to…" And that was when he noticed who she'd been talking to—No-Boundaries Lady from the bar. The one with the daughter. "Hey."

There was literally only one reason she was here, and it wasn't because she'd suddenly become the guardian of a kid in need of pediatric care. She had her sights set on Dr. Eric Carlton for her daughter.

"Hi," she said with a sheepish smile.

"Can I help you? I'm sorry, Miss…" Decency was ingrained, even when the outcome wasn't going to go in his favor.

"Helen. Michaels."

"Yes, the real estate agent. I remember."

He remembered and then some. Now would be a good time to have an emergency interruption. No such luck.

"I was just thinking about our discussion the other night," Helen said. "And I was hoping I could buy you a cup of coffee."

"Helen and I go way back," Donna offered cheerily. "She sold me my house."

The theme music from the It's a Small World ride at Disney World started playing through his head. "You don't say."

Donna pointed out the window. "There's a great coffee shop just down the block."

Okay, no more help needed, Donna, thanks. Just then, the interruption he'd been hoping for materialized in the form of Joey Baldwin, a bespectacled patient with a distal radius fracture that Eric had set last week. The kid had come in for a checkup so they could see how his wrist was healing.

"Doctor Eric," Joey called and held up his cast with undisguised glee. "Will you sign my cast?"

Eric grinned. "You betcha, buddy."

Joey was his favorite patient at the moment for more reasons than one. But mostly because he'd provided a great distraction from the Helen Michaels Ambush happening in his office.

Eric grabbed a marker from Donna's pen cup and motioned the boy over. "You come over here. Let's take a look at this."

Long ago, Eric had taken to drawing pictures on kids' casts as a way to make the whole thing less scary and maybe memorable in a good way. He narrated the drawing as he penned it in. "This is you hitting a home run, coming around first base—"

Joey looked stricken. "But I don't play baseball."

Shoot. Eric should've known that but he was pre-occupied with what he knew was coming from Helen as soon as the coast was clear. "Oh, okay. Well, what do you play?"

"I'm a science nerd," Joey announced proudly.

"Good for you. I was a science nerd. All right. Then this is you winning the Nobel Prize for curing broken arms. Look at that. What do you think?"

"Cool!" Joey glanced at the picture and back up again at Eric, completely thrilled with both the thought and the picture.

And now for the *pièce de résistance*. "I just saw you got a bit of an owie behind your ear. Let me take a look at that."

Eric reached in his pocket and performed the world's worst sleight of hand, producing a sucker from behind Joey's ear, then presented it to him. The kid's eyes lit up like Eric had handed him a million dollars. This was the kind of thing that made being a doctor worth all the insurance snarls and nerve-wracking waits for test results.

"Thank you," Joey called as he galloped back to his mother.

"You're welcome," Eric told him and turned back to Helen and Donna.

Helen immediately pounced. "So, how about it. A quick cup of coffee. I want to pitch you something and if you're not interested, you'll never see me again. You won't regret it."

"You won't," Donna threw in like she had some

idea what Helen was talking about, when in fact, she did not. "Trust her, and she'll find you a home in no time."

And now he was stuck. He couldn't flat-out tell Helen no without raising Donna's suspicions. He'd been working with Donna a long time, and the woman watched after him like a mother hen. She'd badger him to talk to Helen, strictly because she had it in her head that if he was looking for a house, Helen would treat him right.

What was he supposed to do, admit he wasn't looking for a house? That would only invite questions about Helen's real agenda—which he knew good and well had to do with her single daughter—and the less he got Donna involved in his personal life, the better. She did not like Dana and never let him hear the end of it.

If Donna's real estate agent had a daughter, she'd be all over the suggestion for him to call her, shenanigans at The Chameleon Bar notwithstanding.

"Uh…okay." He glanced at his watch as he rifled through his memory for what the rest of his day looked like, schedule-wise. It was pretty packed. "Look, I can meet you in twenty minutes, but just for, like, five minutes."

That would make everyone happy, and he could go back to doing his job.

Helen looked as thrilled as Joey and took herself off toward the elevator. "I'll quit while I'm ahead. Just down the block?"

Donna stood and pointed toward the west end of the hospital. "Just down the block."

So *that* had happened. Eric shook his head and skirted the reception area to head toward exam room three, where he had a patient waiting the requisite fifteen minutes after a vaccination.

Nate, his partner at the practice, was standing there, and apparently he'd watched the whole scene.

"Why can't I ever meet older married women?" he asked with thinly veiled sarcasm.

"Don't start, okay?" Eric warned his friend. "She's a real estate agent. I met her the other night. She probably just wants to sell me something."

"Your secret is safe with me," he stage-whispered, because apparently, he thought he was funny.

It was hilarious, actually. Eric was the guy going to meet a woman's mother so she could try to convince him to meet said woman. Maybe he was the crazy one.

Six

Eric didn't make it to the coffee shop for almost forty-five minutes. He half hoped Helen would give up on him before he appeared, but no. She was still sitting at the counter nursing a cup of coffee.

"Sorry, I'm late," he told her. "A baby with colic and a sleepless mother."

Helen's smile of relief told him she'd been worried he'd stand her up. Like, if he hadn't shown up, that would really affect her and her world. Wow. All of this to get her daughter set up with a random man Helen had met in a bar? It boggled the mind.

This woman was something else. And it told him there was a possibility her daughter had a lot of fortitude: a requirement for putting up with this kind of interference from her mother.

"Claire had colic," Helen said, obviously desperate for some type of connection between her daughter and Eric. Then she seemed to realize that wasn't the bonus she'd made it out to be. "She's over it now. Forgive me. Just a little hyper. I've had two cups of coffee. Okay, let me cut to the chase. I think you should meet my daughter."

Saw that one coming a mile away. Eric took a cup of coffee from the barista with a smile of thanks.

"Yeah, didn't you say the other night that she was going to disown you?" A non-answer if there ever was one. Why hadn't he flat-out said no?

"She doesn't have to know about my involvement. Besides, didn't you say your lips were sealed?"

Touché. "Yes, well. That was when it didn't include me."

"Doctor Carlton. Eric." Helen put her hand on his arm to up the familiarity factor, as if they were all friends here. "All you have to do is cross paths. You'll see. I know these things."

Her attempt to make this seem less like a horrible idea didn't fool him. "You know I was there the other night. I'd say that your batting average is less than stellar."

"Well, they can't all be home runs. But this...this is a sure thing. I just know it is."

Helen really did seem to believe that she was doing the right thing and that there was nothing off-kilter about chasing down a man with the sole intent of finding her daughter a date. It was tripping him up.

"Okay, you've got my curiosity piqued." Against his will. But still. What was this daughter like? Was she *really* in the dark about her mother's shenanigans? He kind of wanted to see for himself what sort of person this mystery woman was. "What is your plan?"

"Well, the other night I overheard that you were going to the fundraiser at the gallery."

Yeah, that reminder put a damper on this coffee shop ambush. "I was going to, but I'm not going now that Dana can't make it."

Things were not progressing with Dana. At all. She'd canceled their date last night, too. He understood the demands of a surgeon better than most, but seriously—even he had to draw the line somewhere, right?

It wasn't that he wanted to own anyone's time, but lots of other surgeons met people and got married. Had relationships that included actually seeing their significant other. Dana could too. She just had to figure out how to balance her work with Eric. Which she hadn't chosen to do thus far. If she didn't think he was worth it, then fine. But she should tell him that instead of stringing him along.

"Well, now you have a reason to go, because Claire is going to be there." Helen paused to let that sink in. "She owns a bakery. Her and her partner have the contract to cater the event. I won't even tell her you're going. Or that I even met you. You go, you meet her, you decide."

It still sounded contrived. "I don't know."

That was putting it mildly.

Helen let him sip his coffee in peace and then offered to walk him back to the office, which he appreciated, because he really wanted to check on the colicky baby. The rain hadn't started yet today, and the walk through the park might've been pleasant if he'd had less chatty company.

On the way, Helen geared up her pitch again. "She's funny and kind, and she puts up with me. Did I mention she's a pastry chef? You'll gain a lot of weight, but you'll die happy."

All points in her daughter's favor. They didn't, however, outweigh the weird factor to all of this.

"You really are relentless," he told her. "Look, I'm not going to say yes, but I will think about it."

What was wrong with him? He wasn't actually considering this half-baked idea, was he? *No.* No, he was not considering it.

It was just...Dana. He was really disappointed about how things were panning out with her. And it was really hard to meet women, even in a city the size of Seattle.

Reverse that. It wasn't that hard. He clearly wasn't putting much effort into it.

"Okay, fair enough," Helen said with a knowing smile, as if she'd gotten him all figured out. "There's just one little hitch. Claire can't ever know we spoke. It's much better if she thinks she just met you by chance."

That was the last straw. "I'm not that comfortable lying."

"Well, it's not a lie," Helen corrected instantly with far too much calculation for his taste. "It's just something to omit. You go to the fundraiser, you meet her, whatever happens, happens."

"I don't know."

That seemed to be his standard answer, when a flat no would be much more clear. Conflict wasn't his strong suit.

It sounded like a disaster waiting to happen. Especially the part about pretending he'd met this woman's daughter by chance. In his world, he couldn't leave anything to chance, not when patient diagnoses lay in the balance. Careful thought processes and precise science—that was what worked in his life. That was the whole reason he'd asked Dana out. They made sense together. When they actually *were* together.

"Look," Helen said as they paused under one of the park pavilions where musicians set up on the weekend. "You seem like a great guy, and she is the most incredible person I know, and I swear I am not just saying that because I am her mother."

This lady seemed so earnest about all of this, as if there really was nothing wrong with railroading a guy into meeting her daughter and then making up some cockamamie story about how he'd seen her across the room and had to speak to her.

"Let me think about it. Okay?"

He wouldn't. It was ludicrous. And he'd spent more than enough time on this nonsense. He had sick patients to heal, and that, he understood. He skedaddled before she came up with even more wonderful accolades on her daughter's behalf.

Helen called after him. "You won't regret it. Promise."

"Goodbye, Helen." For real this time.

The new oven might be Claire's favorite thing in the bakery at the moment. It was beautiful and shiny and just...*beautiful.* She and Marco's white coats reflected in the chrome, which put out this dim glow that seemed to cover the entire kitchen.

Yes, she was being fanciful. So what?

This was a great day, and she was allowed to be happy about the sudden shower of fortune that had come their way.

"For a used oven, it works great," Claire told Marco as he examined the glass doors. "We were lucky to find one with such low hours."

"Too bad it doesn't come with customers."

That was his way of saying he liked it. She smiled. With a new oven in place, anything was possible. The gallery event would open new doors for them. She knew it.

She glanced at a text message from her mother. "Mom said we should go all out for the gallery fundraiser. I'm thinking petit fours."

Claire didn't usually go to such trouble, mostly because petit fours took hours longer than something like coconut lime tarts. But it would be worth it if she did well enough with them to get people to come into the bakery. And executed the coupon idea.

Then they'd have the customers Marco was longing for. She could see it all in her mind as if it had already happened, and maybe that was the universe's way of helping that along.

Marco nodded over his bread dough that would be the inaugural batch baked in their new oven as he considered the idea of petit fours. "Okay, make sure you use the glacé, include the napoleons, and your *millefoglie* is amazing so I'll help you build it—"

"What?" Claire reread the newest text from her mother. It still said the same thing. "She wants me to get my hair cut for the catering gig. What's wrong with my hair?"

Not to mention the fact that it would be up in a bun. Like usual. Otherwise she'd have to wear a hair net, and that was the least attractive thing on the planet.

"Nothing, but it's your mother we're talking about," Marco said with his usual wit.

It wasn't funny, though.

Claire frowned. There was only one reason her mother would mention anything about hair—she had something planned. Maybe she'd contacted the newspaper about the gallery event's caterer and expected Claire's picture to be taken. It was over the line. But if so, it couldn't hurt to use the opportunity to get more publicity, and the better she presented herself as the owner of the bakery, the better chance she had of enticing customers through the door.

A good reminder that she had to act as the face of the bakery since Marco wouldn't be there. But she wasn't getting a haircut.

Eric sat in the breakroom at the back of the office building going over yet another sheaf of paperwork at the end of a long day of patient rounds. Sometimes he sat in his private office, but today, that was too far from the coffee pot, and the paperwork didn't end for a busy doctor.

Nate, who must've just finished up with his last patient as well, came into the room and slapped Eric on the shoulder.

"Hey," Eric said and checked off the proper medical code on the form.

Maybe if he didn't look up, Nate would skip the interrogation about Helen. But he'd known Nate a long time, since medical school.

They were friends first and colleagues second. Which meant the odds of getting lucky enough to escape Nate's good-natured prying into Eric's life were zero.

"So, how did you meet the real estate woman anyway?" Nate called from behind the counter.

"She approached me at the Chameleon while I was waiting for Dana," Eric said evenly and signed the form. Good thing he was almost done.

"Oh yeah, Doctor Becker." Nate might have left off the juvenile *niiiiiice,* but it was implied in his tone. "How's that going?"

"Ehhh." That was the nicest word he could think of for his tepid opinion about Dana lately.

Eric shrugged and went to refill his coffee cup as Nate's eyes practically fell out of his head.

"What, you're not attracted to pretty and smart?"

"Of course I am, but she's kind of…" Eric paused, not sure what word he was looking for to describe what was wrong with Dana. "Cold. Has no sense of humor."

That wasn't what he'd meant to say. He hadn't even realized that part of her personality had been bothering him until this conversation. In fact, he'd have said the only thing wrong with her was her inability to make Eric a priority. Now, he'd uncovered something a lot deeper of a problem.

"Laughter is overrated," Nate deadpanned.

Maybe so. But that was what Eric wanted—a woman he could laugh with. It wasn't a crime. Surely there was a woman out there who'd share his slightly dry sense of humor. Maybe someone who'd had to develop one in order to put up with a giant personality in their inner circle who interfered with this fictional woman's daily life. Like a busybody mother…

Great. Now Nate had Eric wondering what kind of personality Claire Michaels had. Strictly from an academic standpoint. Not because he was seriously considering meeting the woman. But if he was considering it, what kind of person would she be? Did she like kids? Animals? Foreign language films no one else had ever heard of but when he mentioned the title, she'd laugh and say that one was a favorite?

Donna bustled into the breakroom on a mission, and Eric was it. She paused long enough to skewer him with what he privately called her "mom" look, the one she leveled regularly at the two men she worked for. Sometimes he countered it by telling her it made her resemble a young Diana Ross, but the compliment didn't stop her from barging ahead with her agenda.

"So, are you buying?" she asked point blank.

"Um, what?" Eric asked.

"Property. A house. Condo. Whatever."

Oh, that. It was time to nip all of this in the bud.

Eric didn't even like the suggestion that he might have met Helen for any reason other than the real one. Honesty was important to him. Kids could tell when you were lying, especially when they asked if something was going to hurt. It was better to be up-front from the very beginning. That was why his patients trusted him. He'd vowed early on that he'd never even bend the truth, let alone break it.

Everyone deserved that.

"I am not buying a house, and I am not dating the real estate agent." This he directed at Nate before he started in on him again. "She just tried to set me up. Wants me to meet her daughter."

"Well, Helen did right by me all those years ago," Donna said with her typical black-and-white take on things. "I think you should go out with her."

Despite her rather unorthodox approach to getting her daughter a date, Helen seemed to have won over Donna. That was hard to do. Donna didn't suffer fools easily.

"I don't know," Nate said with a dire expression on his face as he stuck his hands in the pockets of his white coat. "I feel like if the daughter is anything like the mom, she is probably crazy."

Yeah, Eric had had that thought too, but all at once, he wanted to defend Claire. After all, Helen had been so clear that her daughter didn't even know her mother was running around soliciting random guys to pretend-meet her.

Like he'd told Helen, he'd be mortified if his mom was doing that. Claire probably would be too, once she found out. Which meant maybe Claire *wasn't* crazy and might be more like the woman her mother had pitched her as. A pastry chef running her own bakery, which meant she was ambitious and smart, as well as busy, which meant she'd understand that he was, too. He'd seen her picture and she was pretty.

"You know what? The way she described her, she actually sounds pretty cool."

"Oh man, don't do it." Nate shook his head with a smirk as he took in Eric's expression. "It's a mistake."

What did his expression look like? A man who'd decided that he might be in the market for a pretty pastry chef after all, one who had enough good humor to put up with a busybody mom?

Donna frowned and pointed in Nate's direction. "This coming from the man who bought his wife a blender for their anniversary."

"I will have you know that was the Cadillac of blenders," Nate told Donna as if that might be some kind of defense against his poor husbanding.

Besides, Nate's wife was devoted to him, and the

blender thing had blown over once he'd taken her to Aruba in apology.

But that was the crux of the matter. Nate and Donna both had someone in their lives. He didn't. And he wanted to meet someone special, which didn't seem to be happening under his own volition.

Eric held up his hands to stem the tide of his co-workers' very strong opinions. "Listen. There's no rush because I have until Saturday, but I really appreciate the concern you have for me."

The sarcasm might have been a little thick. But come on. This was his decision, and he didn't need advice from the peanut gallery. Since he still had a mountain of paperwork to get through, he grabbed his full coffee cup and got on with his super-fun night of forms and ink.

"What?" Donna called after Nate when he shot her a look.

Clearly, they both had their own ideas about what he should do, but he was the only one who could make this choice. Eric wasn't a believer in fate, and he didn't think that Helen had been put in his path by some divine chess player. She'd seen something she wanted for her daughter and had gone after it. He admired that kind of dedication and persistence. Maybe the daughter would have some of that, too..

It couldn't hurt to take thirty minutes, go to the gallery, and see what all the fuss was about. He could satisfy his somewhat piqued curiosity, compliment Claire's desserts, and go on if there was nothing there to keep his interest.

And he could pretend all day long that he wouldn't be giving Nate and Donna a run-down of the event on Monday. But he probably would.

Seven

C LAIRE CAME OUT OF THE Crate and Barrel homewares store across the street from Trevi, the farm-to-table restaurant that had scored a great review by the Wandering Gourmet, which reminded her she needed to try that place. Marco had recommended it highly, which was saying something coming from one of the harshest food critics around. If he liked something, it might as well have been cooked by angels.

She set her bag in the passenger seat of the car and started the engine, her mind going a million miles an hour. She had a ton of work to do for the gallery event and really hadn't had the time to spare, but she'd needed better-quality serving dishes, or the petit fours would end up on boring glass platters with no panache at all.

A sleek black car slid into the spot across from her, right in front of Trevi. That was the only reason she noticed when an extremely good-looking man stepped out. As he headed toward the shops on this side of the street, recognition tingled her skin. Where had she seen him before?

He disappeared inside the homewares shop she'd literally just stepped out of. *Dang*. How was that for bad luck? If she'd been two minutes later, she might've run into him at the checkout line and struck up a casual conversation.

That would be a great story.

Claire shook her head, laughing at herself as she drove away. If she really cared about meeting someone serendipitously, then she should think about a manicure at least, and possibly that haircut advice she'd ignored.

Her mother was really getting to her.

As if she'd somehow conjured her up, Claire's mother came over later that night unexpectedly, carrying a bag from one of the more exclusive retailers in Seattle.

She shot her mom a look. "What is this?"

"An airplane," Helen told her with an eye roll. "What do you think it is? A dress. Try it on."

A dress for what? Her mother was definitely up to something. But Claire couldn't resist peeking at the contents of the bag, because after all, her mother's taste was incredible. It couldn't hurt to at least see what—*Oh, man*.

Claire's breath caught as the black dress unfolded from her fingertips. This was more than a dress. It was destiny waiting to happen. In this dress, she'd meet someone special for sure. But she'd have to be wearing it in order for that to be the outcome, and she had nothing planned that might warrant such a dress.

Regardless, there was no reason she couldn't try it on, right?

It fit like a dream, and as she stepped in front of the full-length mirror, her mother smiled.

"This is going to look great on you at the gallery event tomorrow night," her mom said.

Oh. So that was the plan. "It's beautiful, but I'm just the caterer. I'm not the belle of the ball."

She couldn't wear this to the gallery event. It would have flour all over it in no time flat. But still... if her mother had organized some kind of surprise publicity, a theory that was sounding more and more plausible given the mounting evidence, Claire would definitely wow in this dress.

Helen waved off Claire's objections anyway. "This is an important event, and besides, I got it on sale. I couldn't resist."

That made it practically a requirement to wear, then. There were rules about these sort of things, and a dress on sale meant the universe had decided this would be Claire's attire for the gallery event. "Thank you, but you shouldn't have."

"You're a vision. Now what are you going to do for shoes?"

Ugh, she hadn't even thought that far ahead. She'd have to wear something practical since she'd be on her feet the whole night. "I have those open-toed pumps."

"Oh no, those are so plain. That dress requires a new pair of shoes."

It did. It really did. But *gah*, how could she justify spending that kind of money on a catering event outfit? She'd already spent the event deposit on a new oven. "Maybe."

Her mother just gave her a look. "Not maybe. *Yes.* That's the only word that needs to come out of your mouth for the next twenty-four hours. Trust me."

The genteel gallery crowd wandered through the maze of stark-white walls viewing the artwork, their conversation muted and indiscernible. Claire didn't have to hear their comments about the paintings. The only thing she cared about was whether they liked her desserts, and judging by the low inventory on every tray, they did.

The gallery director, a high-strung woman by the name of Brenda Chang, jetted over, her straight dark hair swinging wildly. She surveyed the table as if trying to gauge whether there were enough to last—and there were, thank you, because the caterer knew how to do her job—then nodded at Claire.

"I wish the event was as big a hit as your desserts. I'll gain five pounds if I don't watch myself," Brenda said.

Claire smiled at the compliment. "Well, I'm glad you like them. I also have a restaurant downto—"

"Hold that thought."

Brenda darted after one of the patrons, an elderly lady encrusted with diamonds. Too bad Brenda hadn't motioned the woman in this direction. Claire's bakery could use a wealthy fan or two.

She glanced past Brenda, her gaze landing on the man behind her. A sudden jolt rocked her spine. The same jolt she'd gotten before, but this time she *knew* she recognized him.

Time slid to a stop, and the people, the artwork, the chatter, all of it, faded as he walked toward her, his gaze similarly fastened on her. There was practically music playing in her head. Okay, well, there really *was* music piping from the sound system, but somehow he made it a whole other kind of moment, one full of magic and fairytale glitter.

"Hi," he murmured, and his voice...

Oh, yes, his voice was amazing and deep and it thrilled through her, raising goosebumps in its wake.

"Hi."

How she got that out around the huge, sudden lump in her throat, she'd never know.

It's the guy. The one from Crate and Barrel.

And here he was in the flesh, talking to her and even better-looking in the low gallery light in a crisp suit that looked *amazing* on him. She might have to find a way to surreptitiously fan herself, because *wow*.

"So, how's your night going?" he asked.

"Good." Fabulous, she wasn't squeaking out her answers like a squirrel with stage fright.

He held out a hand. "I'm Eric."

"Claire."

She shook his hand, and everything inside her collided in a mess of destiny, squishy-girl feelings that only happened when you met someone worth squishing over, and a giddy sense of wonder. Providence had finally smiled down on her. This was a moment she'd remember for a long time.

To wrap everything up in a big, solid bow, he seemed to have come to the fundraiser alone and didn't seem to be in any hurry to go elsewhere.

"Are you an art aficionado?" he asked with a nod toward the wall behind that held a very ugly Robachaux painting from what appeared to be the artist's messy finger-paint period, inexplicably titled "Eggplant with No Fur."

"Do I lose points if I say the jury is still out?"

Eric's smile came slowly but it was worth it, like waiting for the sun to break out from behind the clouds. The intensity of it washed over her. She'd always been a rain girl—had to be, to live in this town—but all at once, she became a huge fan of Eric's warm rays.

"Actually, I've been glancing around and I gotta say…" He leaned in, wafting her with a heavy dose of masculinity she couldn't help but react to, and murmured, "You're wise to withhold judgement until you've seen all of it. Want to walk around with me and let's decide together?"

She couldn't help it. She shivered. The good kind, the kind full of anticipation, like when you knew the wrapped box in front of you held the present you'd longed for, but you hadn't opened it yet because wanting it was too much fun.

Unfortunately, she wasn't a guest. "I can't. I'm the caterer, so I'm kind of stuck here. I can circulate with trays, but my time is limited."

Which was exactly the way she wanted it. The tiny ping of disappointment had no place in the middle of a gig that had bought her and Marco a new oven.

His intense gaze never wavered from hers. "I'll wait."

Really? Like, how long? Until the event was done? "That might be a while. At least until all of the desserts are gone."

"Well. That sounds like a challenge." He glanced behind him and called out, "Wow, these desserts are incredible. Where can I find more?"

A few people heard him. Hard not to when his voice carried like a Broadway actor. There was a brief pause as some of the glances shifted in her direction, as if they were waiting for her answer. "Oh. I actually have a restaurant downtown."

Eric picked up another petit four and ate it in one bite, then spoke over his shoulder. "You don't say. What is it called?"

Holy cow. He was trying to get people into her bakery. And to eat her desserts. There might be some seriously giddy swooning in her future.

"It's called Gilded Sweets Bakery," she replied.

"Great name." That was directed toward her, along with one of his signature smiles, which she was becoming quite fond of. "Do you have any cards?"

"As a matter of fact, I do."

She pulled out one and handed it to him, thrilled to the marrow at how skillfully he was playing this game. And for what? Just so she'd have time to walk around and look at the art with him? It was unbelievable. Perfect.

The story formed in her head almost automatically. *The day we met, he goaded an entire roomful of people into eating all my desserts so he could have my attention faster.* Delicious.

"Ooh, three twenty-six Franklin Street," he said to the room at large.

A woman with a fall of dark-brown hair behind him piped up. "May I have a card?"

He glanced at Claire with a knowing look and handed his over. "You can have this one. I'll get another one."

"These petit fours are pretty unique," she said as she surveyed the selection. Her presence at the table seemed to get other guests moving toward them, and soon, several people had drifted over to chow down.

"Thank you," Claire said with genuine gratefulness as she watched all her hard work being devoured. "I use almond extract to counter the sweetness."

"All of the desserts are quite exceptional," the lady said as she picked up one more with marked interest, scrutinizing it from all sides. "I'll have to stop by sometime."

"Great." Claire waited until she'd walked a good distance away and then lowered her voice so only Eric could hear her. "You have to stop doing that. I'm going to run out of cards."

He didn't even bother to look chagrined. "I'll have you know I'm expecting some kind of kickback."

"Okay, well, you know where I am. Come in anytime you want. All the pastries you can eat, on the house."

It was a great way to invite him to the bakery without being overly obvious. Though it didn't really seem as if this was one of those times when she needed to play it cool. Eric was clearly interested in her. Wonder of wonders. It was almost miraculous.

"Great," he said with another smile that seemed to be a part of his permanent expression. "It's really thinned out in here. Maybe we can take a look at some art now."

Claire didn't see Brenda anywhere, and her table was almost bare. It wouldn't hurt to vanish for a little while, would it? No one had to know there was a whole second batch back in the service area.

She wanted to spend some more time with this unexpected man who'd dropped out of nowhere. Who was she to tempt the fates? "Sure."

This catering gig *had* turned out to be the start of something amazing. But even she couldn't have predicted that Eric would be the icing on that petit four.

Eight

THERE WAS ABSOLUTELY NOTHING WRONG with Claire, and her mother had a lot of nerve being so over the top about getting Eric to go out with her. He'd almost missed out on meeting this fabulous woman simply because Helen had oversold it.

That would've been a crying shame.

Thank goodness he'd ignored Nate and come to the gallery fundraiser anyway. This was shaping up to be the best move he'd made in a long time. All because of Claire. Unexpected, beautiful Claire Michaels.

He and Claire stood in front of a giant swirl of primary colors, but his attention wasn't on the artwork. It was on her. She smelled amazing, a combination of vanilla, sugar, and something vaguely fruity that might be apples but could be pear.

This was the first time he could remember being so utterly captivated by someone. The artwork could hardly compare, and he didn't care a bit if she clued in that he'd been hit crossways by her.

But because they were supposed to be "looking at

art," he had to say something about the blobby paint-ing they were standing in front of.

"What do you see?" he asked her, keenly interested to get another glimpse into her mind.

Claire scarcely paused for a millisecond. "I see the weird face of a yellow man about to eat a fish."

He bit back a smile since she didn't seem to be kidding, but yeah. Well put.

"While standing in a burning forest," he offered.

Claire laughed softly, a sound he didn't think he could get enough of.

"It's open for interpretation, I guess," she said gra-ciously.

"Yes, that's the point."

One he liked enormously at the moment, because it afforded him an opportunity to have this art in-terpretation conversation with Claire. He could talk about art all day long if it prolonged their interaction.

"I have been on my feet all day and these are new shoes," Claire confessed and crossed to the lone bench along the south wall of the room.

Without hesitation, she slipped off her black pumps and rested her feet flat on the concrete floor with an expression of pure relief. He could hardly look away from her face. She was so expressive, so animated. So beautiful.

What was wrong with the men of Seattle that this woman's mother had to chase down interested parties in order to get Claire on a date? It was baffling.

"Oh, my gosh," Claire said, her voice rich with undisguised pleasure as she called over her shoulder.

"You should take your shoes off. Art is so much better barefoot."

The expression on her face as she stared at the painting placed prominently in front of the bench said otherwise. Maybe she'd meant the experience of art was better. Not the art itself. Frankly, most of the stuff in this gallery made no sense to him.

"Do you like that one?" he asked her, curious what she'd say.

"I prefer pieces that depict the human condition."

"Such as?"

"Edward Hopper, Winslow Homer, Georgia O'Keeffe. Artists that break your heart in the best way." She glanced up as he joined her on the bench. "What about you?"

"Oh, I am super corny. I don't usually divulge that type of information on a first date."

But he most definitely would on a second date. He had to hold something back to entice her into going out with him. There was no way he'd pass up the opportunity to see where this thing could go.

"Presumptuous."

"Is it?"

He didn't think so. If a date was two people at an event who liked each other, wanted to spend time together, and hoped to get to know each other better, this was one times a thousand.

She laughed, apparently in agreement with his unspoken thoughts. "Come on. I swear I won't judge."

"Norman Rockwell. I like the way he captures children."

This was the litmus test. A very personal revelation that would set the tone for their future. Because if she didn't like kids, he was out.

"I completely agree. He really captures people's innocence."

Good answer. Great. The best. She had this optimism he couldn't help but be attracted to, especially as it came out in the most intriguing ways.

Footsteps echoed from the second story landing, and a female voice rang out from above their heads.

"We're closing now." A dark-haired woman leaned over the balcony railing to call down to them. "I wanted to thank you and let you know I'll be using you again."

"Great," Claire called.

"She's got a little bakery downtown," Eric informed her, still keeping up with the earlier game.

Because he wanted to and he could. What was the point of being in a relationship with someone if you weren't there to lift each other up? Sure, it was early. But he planned to do everything in his power to continue getting to know Claire.

"I'll be sure to stop by," the lady said.

"Three twenty-six Franklin," he threw in.

As Claire laughed at his antics, the woman said, "Say hi to your mom."

"I will."

The woman vanished from the landing, leaving them alone again.

"My mom got me this gig," Claire explained, seeming flustered. "I really should pack up."

Since he well knew how Helen pulled the strings of Claire's life, he got it. Probably far more than he should.

She stood, and Eric did too. Without her heels, she was shorter. More easily folded into an embrace, he couldn't help but think.

"Okay. Well, let me help you," he insisted.

"Oh. That's absolutely not necessary."

What, people didn't help each other in her world? "I'd like to."

She nodded her agreement, and he followed her to the serving area in the back of the gallery, where it looked like a disaster relief center. "Where should I start?"

Pointing, Claire got him busy stacking dishes into the boxes she'd brought and then asked him to carry them outside to her little red Mini Cooper. He'd noticed a similar one at Crate and Barrel yesterday, but only because it had a distinctive white stripe down the center.

There were probably hundreds of red Mini Coopers around. The odds of accidentally running into Claire while out shopping were zero. But it was funny to think of the irony if he had met her by chance.

Funny in a not-so-funny way. If he'd met Claire yesterday, he could've left Helen completely out of the picture, and then that guilty secret wouldn't be weighing down his shoulders.

Now that he'd met Claire...what was he supposed to do about acknowledging her mother's schemes? Did he even need to? Couldn't he let it ride for a while longer until something happened that made him think otherwise? They'd literally just met. No need to assign more importance to it with heavy confessions.

Claire supervised the placement of the boxes in her trunk, slipping her hands into the pockets of her long coat she'd donned to brave the elements outside. The streets had a wet sheen to them that meant it had rained while he'd been inside being bowled over by Claire.

"Thanks so much for your help," she said, her voice dropping a little into a textured register that did a number on him.

"You bet." He shut the double hatch doors firmly as it started drizzling again. "So, what do you do with all of the leftovers?"

"Well, unfortunately, they don't really keep."

"You don't throw them out, do you?"

"Sadly, that's often what happens, yeah."

He moved over a bit as she rounded the rear of the car to give her enough room. Not much room, because he liked being close to her. She leaned a hip on the rear of the car as she gazed up him with a somber twist to her mouth.

He preferred it when she smiled. He preferred it even more when he gave her a reason.

"I know someone that would absolutely love those. It might be a little unorthodox. But it will be worthwhile. Just might be the best part of your evening."

"I don't know if that's possible," she said with a tiny head shake.

A long look passed between them as he contemplated all the ways to interpret that statement. Judging by the glint in her eyes, he wouldn't be off base to assume she meant she'd been enjoying their time together. That was a very nice development indeed, one that set off an explosion of warmth in his chest.

"But," she continued, and there came that smile he was really starting to crave. "I'm willing to give it a shot."

"Okay, great."

By tacit agreement, she climbed into the driver's seat of her red car, and he took the passenger seat. Eric gave her directions to the hospital, which she followed flawlessly, another point in her favor. It wouldn't be a no if she'd turned out to be a horrible driver or bad with directions, but there was something unexpectedly attractive about a woman who was confident behind the wheel.

"We're visiting a patient?" Claire asked as she pulled into the visitor's lot.

If he'd known they were coming, he'd have brought his ID badge so they could park in the covered doctor's lot, but this was literally the last place he'd expected to be tonight. And literally the last person he'd have guessed would be accompanying him.

He hadn't told her where they were going on purpose.

"Yeah. Is that okay?"

Another litmus test. This was where he spent the majority of his time: with kids who needed his help to get better. If she couldn't handle the doctor part of him, it was better to know that now.

"I just wanted to find out if we were passing out leftovers to your colleagues or sick kids. Because your doctor friends can come to the bakery," she said with a wink. "Kids can't."

"Exactly."

A nurse in pink scrubs stood by the patient's bedside, checking her temperature. She smiled when she caught sight of Eric and quickly vacated the room so he and Claire could come in. Someone had brought Emily a cache of cheerful balloons sometime since earlier today. Her mom, likely, who'd scarcely left her daughter's side.

They'd run into her in the hall, and he'd suggested she take a short break while Eric and Claire visited, which the frazzled mom had gratefully taken them up on. She'd been at the hospital since that morning with barely a second to grab something to eat.

It was telling, what moms were willing to do for their children. Now that Eric had met Claire, he saw Helen's interference a little differently. Not much, but a little. Her tactics were still in question, but she wasn't necessarily irrational. At least, not all the way.

Emily lit up as Eric came into the small room. She looked a lot better than she had when she'd come in, that was for sure. He glanced at her chart even though he wasn't on call. She was steady. That was great news.

"Hi, Dr. Carlton," she called.

"Hi, Emily," he said as he moved over to the far

side of the hospital bed to take a seat. "This is my friend Claire."

"Hi, Emily," Claire said and didn't hesitate to follow him, sitting at the end of Emily's bed with no question, even without being told what Emily was in the hospital for or if it was communicable.

That lodged in his heart sideways.

"Hi. I got stung by a bee. I'm allergic," Emily explained. "I got all swolled up."

"But you're going to be just fine," Eric interjected before anyone got a different idea. "We brought you some yummy treats."

"How come?"

"Because you are such a brave girl."

Emily looked confused. "I was? My mom says I'm a handful."

Sure, because Emily had gotten stung climbing a tree at a neighbor's house and had neglected to bring her epi-pen with her, even though her mother had reminded her twice. He'd gotten that tearful story this morning once Emily's vitals had stabilized.

"Well, you're a brave handful," he amended.

"Do you want to try one?" Claire asked with a nod at the leftover desserts in her hand.

Emily nodded and sat up.

Claire flipped open the box's lid and held it out for the little girl to survey.

"Okay, take your pick. Oh, good choice," she said softly as Emily selected an éclair, then watched the little girl bite into it.

"Did you make this?" Emily's expression could

only be described as blissful with a side of *no way*, like it was hard for her to believe such a thing.

"I did."

"They're really good. Thank you."

Emily motioned her forward and kissed her cheek.

Claire looked like she was about to melt under the little girl's attention. "Aww. Thank you. How about I bring you some more tomorrow? Would you like that?"

Emily nodded vigorously as Eric rubbed at the stuck place in his heart. He'd seen Dana with patients a few times at the hospital, and the scene had never struck him as particularly warm. And those were Dana's *patients*, not random kids who'd been dropped on her by a man she'd just met. Claire seemed to naturally know exactly what to say and do despite zero affiliation with Emily other than because Eric had brought her here.

She'd passed all of his litmus tests with flying colors and then some.

"You can finish all of these if you want to," Claire said.

His work here was done. But his relationship with Claire wasn't. Not by a long shot.

Nine

THE LAST THING CLAIRE WANTED to do was get out of bed in the morning. It was far too delicious to stay under the covers and dream about the surprising, amazing, wonderful thing that had happened to her yesterday.

Eric.

He was...well, she didn't know what he was yet. But watching him with Emily had put the cap on it. She wanted to get to know him better. Dive beneath the surface and find out what had inspired him to work with kids. Along the way, she'd see if he'd also treat her with that level of consideration and attention.

Judging by the way he'd focused on her last night with such intensity, she was pretty sure the answer was yes.

But she had a bakery to run, and that didn't mean lounging around in bed, even when she'd had the success of last night's catering job to hopefully benefit from today. If she'd done it right, the gallery patrons would wander the way of Gilded Sweets and bring a much-needed influx of customers.

She climbed from bed and walked to the bakery in the pre-dawn hours, as usual, but yawning this time because she hadn't gone to bed at a reasonable hour, and she wasn't sorry. Marco showed up about thirty minutes after she walked through the door, a new record. He usually came in much later, but the new oven had put a spring in his step that had been missing thus far.

She liked seeing him a little more encouraged.

Time passed in a blur, and as she started working on a new ganache she'd developed, she heard Marco talking to her mom.

Then Helen breezed into the kitchen wearing heels and pearls, so she'd likely come straight from a house showing.

"Hi, sweetheart," she called and rounded the granite slab table where Claire had spread out the chocolate so she could work with it.

"Hi, Mom."

Not a surprise to see her. Helen was here to ask about the gallery event, of course, since she'd coordinated it. Claire should've called her last night to give her the news that it had gone well, but hadn't had time, for obvious reasons that she had no intention of sharing with her mother.

Eric was her secret. For now.

"Brenda Chang called me and said you did a great job," Helen announced and sat on the lone high-backed chair that flanked the table.

Called it in one. "Oh?"

"Did you have a good time?"

"I did," Claire told her, letting all the color of the night infuse her voice. "Except my feet were killing me. I had to take off my new shoes. I was just walking around the gallery barefoot."

The fact that she'd done it with Eric was the highlight she'd be keeping to herself. Her mom didn't have to know about *everything* that went on in Claire's life. And whatever had happened with Eric was too new. Maybe he wouldn't call. Maybe she wouldn't call him. There was no reason to get her mom's hopes up until there was something to tell.

"That's it?" Helen's smile froze. "That's the highlight of your evening?"

"Pretty much," Claire said with careful consideration, as if it hadn't occurred to her to pick a favorite moment from a catering gig.

Which was all it had been, as far as Helen knew.

"That's it? That's all you have to tell me?"

Claire went back to her ganache before it cooled too much. Whatever her mother was fishing for, she didn't have it. "I mean, I didn't really think much of the art."

After a short silence, her mother said, "I'm glad the job went well. Maybe it will bring in some fresh customers."

"Maybe it will."

Claire went to the front to get the chalkboard, where she wrote the day's specials before they opened for brunch, shooting Marco a conspiratorial smile as she passed him. Of course she'd told him all about Eric—and her intense desire to keep it quiet so he didn't accidentally slip to her mom. The second her mother heard Claire had met someone, Helen would start naming the yet-to-be-conceived grandchildren. That was the quickest way to take the magic out of meeting Eric that Claire could think of.

Helen peered at Marco.

"I know nothing," he said dutifully, which was almost the same as admitting that he did know something.

Claire shook her head. She'd tell her mom when there was something to tell, and not a moment before.

On Monday morning, Donna came into the break-room with that no-nonsense look on her face that said she wasn't budging until she heard all the details.

"Okay, okay," Eric said. "You were right. I really liked her."

"I knew it," Donna exclaimed as Nate's ears perked up. "Tell us everything."

Eric poured a cup of coffee he'd clearly need for fortification. Mostly because he wasn't sure how much he wanted to say about the brand-new thing that had blossomed inside him the moment he'd seen Claire across the gallery.

"There's actually not that much to tell," he hedged. "We met at the gallery, got to know each other a little bit, then took leftover pastries to kids at the hospital."

He still couldn't quite believe the evening had unfolded like it had. Perfectly. Exactly as he'd have hoped.

"Sounds like my kind of date," Nate said with his usual bite of sarcasm.

Donna shushed him. "Don't listen to him. I think it sounds romantic."

"It actually really was."

That was the other thing he couldn't reconcile. He'd taken other women he'd dated to the most expensive restaurants, to the top of the Space Needle where the city lay quietly below them in a shower of lights and movement, to the beach at Alki where the views of the water were unparalleled. And yet an impromptu tour of an art gallery and quick side trip to visit sick kids had been the best date of his life.

It just showed that spending money on someone wasn't the key to figuring out whether you liked them enough to see them again.

Nate, not to be outdone by Eric's rebuttal, shot him an incredulous look. "And she's okay with her mother choosing her dates for her?"

"Well that's the problem." Eric sipped his coffee as he contemplated all the ways it was not okay. "She actually doesn't know that yet."

It hadn't come up. Or, more to the point, he hadn't brought it up. In his defense, he'd had no idea Claire was going to captivate him like she had. Instantly. Irrevocably. Unfortunately, it had been too late the second their gazes had met across the room.

Yet he couldn't be sorry he'd taken Helen's suggestion to meet her daughter at the gallery event Claire had catered. That was the reason things had gone so well—it had forced him to be creative in how he got a bit of her attention. And had reaped enormous benefits.

"Uh-oh." Donna shook her finger at him with full-on mom face. "That is a problem."

"I told you it wasn't going to work," Nate said with a laugh.

Which wasn't helpful. In fact, it brought home the fact that Eric *did* want it to work. A lot. Surely Claire would be forgiving of both her mother's interference and Eric's involvement in the scheme once she knew. Right?

Although, even Helen had said Claire would kill her if she found out her mother had poked her nose in her daughter's dating life again. But there was no reason to believe Claire would lump Eric in with her mother as a co-conspirator. Despite that, he had the distinct sensation it wasn't entirely cool that Claire didn't know everything there was to know in this situation.

"What are you going to do?" Donna asked in all seriousness because she at least got that he was in the throes of a very serious moral dilemma.

"I don't know." Maybe he didn't have to do anything right this minute. He hadn't even called her yet. "I'm sure it will work itself out."

But as he started to leave the breakroom, both Nate and Donna's expressions did not give him a warm fuzzy feeling.

"What?" he said with feigned innocence he probably hadn't pulled off.

After all, he did plan on calling her. Which meant he had to figure out how to assuage the vague feeling that he needed to address the elephant between him and Claire.

Really, he was pretty blameless in the whole thing. All he'd done was meet Claire because his receptionist's real estate agent had mentioned her daughter would be catering an event he'd already planned to go to. So if you really got down to brass tacks, he'd met a woman through mutual friends. That was perfectly legitimate, and Claire would most likely think so too. Once he explained it.

There was no reason to believe Claire would even care how they'd met.

Marco and Claire took a much-needed break early one morning to get coffee from the independently owned place down the street that not only served the best brew, but also sold funky local artwork and collectibles. As fellow small-business owners, Claire and Marco tried to frequent non-chain spots as much as possible, and in reciprocation, the other owners came into Gilded Sweets. Every little bit of business helped, and none of them wanted to see each other eaten by giant conglomerates.

Claire glanced up as Marco handed her a tall white cup with a green lid. "Thank you."

Their bench spot afforded the best view of the city, where she still felt like a part of the bustle and flow but she and Marco could actually talk. Decompress. They'd been so busy lately.

"Great news," he said with something approaching cheer. "We actually made more than we spent yesterday."

They'd had a better-than-average crowd nearly the whole day, but she'd been afraid to ask how the numbers had panned out. In case she'd gauged it wrong. Apparently, she hadn't. "That's fantastic."

"For the first time, like…ever, I actually feel like we have a fighting chance."

She couldn't help but smile, but then lately, that felt like her default expression. "Careful. You're starting to sound like an optimist."

"Well, if we keep filling up the place like we have the past couple of days, you can call me whatever you want." He sipped his coffee and then raised his brows as if he'd remembered something he'd meant to bring up. "Speaking of customers, is it my imagination or have we become, like, the hot spot for the medical community?"

That widened her smile.

"Yeah, I noticed that. I think it's Eric. I think he's sending people our way. It's really sweet."

Her voice drifted off a little as Eric consumed her thoughts—again—which Marco did not miss.

"You like this guy."

It wasn't a question, and he didn't mean it in the

literal sense, because of course she liked him as a person. He was kind and worked with kids. What Marco was trying to get her to admit was that she'd already started falling for him.

Sure, she had a bit of a crush. Who wouldn't? But they'd only met like five minutes ago.

"I don't know." She shrugged, loathe to jinx the specialness of Eric by talking about him. "Maybe. It's just so romantic how we met at the gallery, but I'm still getting to know him, so time will tell."

What if the magic didn't stick? What if they went on a real date and it turned out the other night had been a fluke? Or not as amazing as she remembered it?

The worst part was that she'd always talked to her mom about everything. But lately, Helen had been so...*determined* to fix Claire up, almost to the point of driving a wedge between them. Claire hated that she felt that way, but it didn't change the fact that she needed some space from her mother's meddling.

"I'm just shocked Helen had nothing to do with it," Marco said, which was no joke.

"I know, can you believe it? She's going to kill me when she finds out."

That was practically an admission in and of itself. The only reason her mother would care that Claire hadn't mentioned Eric yet would be because their relationship had gotten serious. Which it hadn't.

"Uh, wait a minute. You haven't told her yet?"

"No, are you kidding me? You know how she is. Besides, I love that we met by chance." There was a whole mystical, wonderful story wrapped up in it that she didn't want to share yet. "So for now, Helen can wait. C'mon, back to work."

Ten

HELEN WAS SUPPOSED TO BE across town in fifteen minutes so she could show the Mayer family a two-story Craftsman that had come on the market. It was within walking distance to the elementary school, the number-one thing on their wish list, so she had a feeling they'd move fast on it.

But instead of getting behind the wheel of her Volvo like a good girl, she'd camped out under the pavilion near the medical building where Eric worked. Yeah, she wasn't totally oblivious to how creepy it was to stalk a man her daughter may or may not have met at the gallery fundraiser, but Helen had no clue either way, because Claire hadn't said a word.

Maybe Eric hadn't bothered to show up. If he hadn't, she wanted to know *why*.

Had he not heard all the great things Helen had mentioned about Claire? Because she could give him the rundown in under a minute flat and be on the road to Beacon Hill before the Mayer family even realized she was a teensy bit late.

She glanced at her watch. It was lunch time, and

she had it on good authority from Donna that he usually walked by here on the way to the sandwich shop at the end of the block, near the coffee place where they'd met last week. But if he didn't hurry, she'd have to come back tomorrow and she'd already wasted an hour yesterday waiting for him. Surely, he wouldn't skip lunch two days in a row.

Thank her lucky stars—there he was, head down over his cell phone.

"Fancy meeting you here," she called out.

Eric glanced up and around for the source of the voice, his gaze zeroing in on her as recognition registered on his face a second before his expression turned into somewhat of a smirk.

"Yeah, what're the odds?"

She did like his slightly sarcastic wit, especially when she deserved it.

"Sorry, I was in the neighborhood." Which wasn't much of an apology. Or the truth. "I just had to know what happened with Claire. She hasn't mentioned it, and I can't ask."

Well, she kind of could. She could casually ask something along the lines of, *Met anyone new?* But honestly, she wanted Claire to *want* to talk to her about what was going on in her life.

Her daughter had been surprisingly closed-mouthed lately. Sure, they did all of the same stuff together, but it felt...different. They were drifting apart, and she had no idea why. It was killing her.

"Seriously, you just need to let this thing go," Eric said noncommittally, which almost turned Helen's back molars to dust as hard as she gritted them together.

"I promise. I will, I just need to know what happened."

As long as Eric had met Claire and things were going well, she could back off. Probably.

But then Eric hesitated so long that Helen had a bad moment. A quadrillion of worst-case scenarios scrolled through her head: she'd scared him off. Or Eric had gotten an emergency phone call from a patient and ended up not going to the event after all. Maybe he'd gone, but Claire had been horrible to him when they'd met.

No. Not that last one. There was no way.

And then Eric half smiled in this goofy way that turned Helen's heart to mush. Because she knew what he was going to say.

"I liked her," he admitted.

She couldn't help it. She spun around with glee she flat-out couldn't contain. "I knew it. So, you hit it off?"

"As far as I was concerned, yeah."

Oh, goodness. That was the best news ever. Of course they'd hit it off. Eric was a dreamboat, and Claire was an incredible woman any man would be thrilled to meet. In fact, men should be lining up to get to Claire, and she'd never understand why they weren't, but no matter. Eric was the one. She could feel it.

Except, he hadn't said Claire felt the same way.

What if Claire hadn't liked him? *Ugh*. Her daughter could be a real ding-dong about men sometimes.

"So, what's the problem?" Helen asked, almost afraid of the answer.

Eric didn't even blink. "Honestly, her mother."

Wow. Claire really did like him.

"That's true," she said, nodding and backing off. Besides, she was late, anyway. "You're right. I'm leaving. I was never here. We never had this conversation."

That last bit echoed around the pavilion as she scurried through it toward her car. The relief coursing through her couldn't be more welcome. Claire would be happy with Eric, and that was enough for Helen. For now.

"I'm serious, Helen," he called after her.

"I think you should call her," she yelled back over her shoulder, in case he needed more positive reinforcement.

"You're the problem," he reiterated. Firmly.

"Okay, bye. Don't forget to call her."

And she didn't even glance back to see if he was at least pulling his phone out. He'd call Claire. She could tell these things.

Eric had planned on calling Claire anyway, but he wished he'd done it before Helen's ambush. Now he had her voice in the back of his head, urging him to pick up the phone, and when he finally did, he didn't want it to come across as having been motivated by her mother's interference.

But then, that ship had sailed. If he'd been so worried about Claire feeling like her mother had manipulated his interest in her, he should never have gone to the gallery.

He was glad he'd gone, though. And glad he'd called Claire to ask her to drop by El Fuego for a quick bite to eat. If they met at the restaurant, it kept things low-key. They weren't exactly dating, not yet, and that gave him a pass on dealing with the mother issue.

If things went as well as he hoped, they could plan something a little splashier. Then see how things would shake out on a planned date.

For now, it was better to take it slow, be sure Claire was worth all of the messy behind-the-scenes stuff he'd eventually have to confess.

El Fuego wasn't terribly crowded, so it was easy to spot Claire when her red Mini Cooper slid into a parking spot. Not that he'd been anxiously watching for her through the plate glass window or anything. Mostly he'd been curious if she'd be the type to show up early or late.

She'd been right on time.

Of course, the second she stepped through the door of the restaurant, his pulse sped up and he had a feeling that no matter what time she'd arrived, it would've been right. He wasn't even going to pretend he wasn't already completely enthralled by her.

"Hi," he murmured as she moved into his space.

"Hi, yourself. This is a nice place," she said, but her gaze was on him.

She hadn't even glanced around once in order to have arrived at any particular conclusion, so he chose to take it the way he hoped she'd meant it. The restaurant was incidental. The company, on the other hand, made it worth her time.

"I hope you're hungry," he said as she nodded vigorously.

"I am. I've been up since dawn and skipped lunch. We're mysteriously overwhelmed with customers lately." Claire raised a brow. "You wouldn't know anything about that, would you?"

"I would absolutely know about that. You run a fabulous bakery that deserves to be successful. Where's the mystery?"

She shot him a grin that made his chest warm. Though probably that was the heat from the open kitchen. It was nice to know that the colleagues he'd been sending her direction had taken him up on the suggestion to check out the bakery.

Clearly she knew he was behind it, but he wasn't the type to take credit for anything like that. It was her amazing pastries that kept them coming back, after all.

"Shall we find a table?" he suggested.

"Sure."

She let him lead the way to a table in the center of the room, where the uptown vibe of El Fuego could be fully experienced, and as soon as the waitress took their order, he caught her gaze. "You should be eating lunch."

"Concern for my health, Doctor?" she responded playfully, a quality of hers he was quickly coming to appreciate.

"Of course. If you pass out from hunger, then your customers will suffer," he told her with a wink. "We can't have that."

"It's a good thing you're feeding me, then."

In a case of the world's best timing, the waitress brought their orders, placing them on the red-and-white checkered table with a smile. Claire dug in, another quality of hers he liked. She did everything with a sense of gusto, and he couldn't stop being attracted to it if he tried.

Claire made a little noise of appreciation. "This is the best and the messiest burger I think I've ever had. How'd you find this place?"

"Well, the owner's daughter was a patient of mine, and he insisted I come down here and try it out. I've been hooked ever since."

"Okay, I have to ask. I'm curious. Why pediatrics?"

A legit question, one he'd like to have a fancier answer to, but he wasn't a complicated guy. "Well, I think it's because that's what I've always wanted to be since I was a kid. What about you? Why pastry chef?"

Claire, on the other hand, settled in as if starting her favorite story.

"When I was a kid, my mom used to let me help

her make dinner, and dessert was by far the most fun to make, and I don't know…"

Her face took on this glow as she talked, and he literally could not peel his gaze from her. Somehow, French fries ended up in his mouth, but he wasn't quite sure how they'd gotten there.

"Cookies became brownies," she continued. "Brownies became cupcakes, cupcakes became tarts, on and on until the kitchen was the best place in the house. I think that's where my favorite moments from childhood were."

That was a good story. Much better than his boring, scientific approach to becoming a pediatrician. He'd studied, gone to lots of classes, and completed his residency. There hadn't been a lot of fanfare, just hard work. That was how he'd gained everything of value in his life.

"I know it's just pastries, but for me," she said, almost apologetically, "it's a form of expression."

Her pastries were far from ordinary, which he could say from experience, but even if he'd never had one, it was clear she'd found her passion. And he hadn't missed that Helen had played a part in forming her daughter's future.

Funny how that seemed to have continued well into Claire's adulthood.

Helen was a force to be reckoned with, as he well knew. But this was the first time he'd fully acknowledged that if things continued with Claire, eventually he'd have to accept that Helen would likely always be in the middle of things.

That business with stalking him to find out whether he'd met Claire or not—her heart had been in the
right place, sure. But it was a little much. Was that the
kind of thing he had to look forward to? Maybe.

And maybe Claire would be worth it.

"Well, I'm no expert," he said, "but I can tell you
that you're really good at what you do."

"Thank you."

He was dying to know more. Mostly to hear her
talk. She had the best voice.

"What about the restaurant? How'd that tran-
spire?"

"Well, I went to go look at places to rent, and
Marco, my business partner, showed up at the exact
same time as I did. We both couldn't afford the place
on our own, so we became partners. It was just meant
to be."

"Or," he offered, "it was just good timing."

Coincidence, if you like. He certainly wasn't a
subscriber to fate. Things worked out like they should
due to hard work, a solid plan, and good follow-
through. If life truly did unfold due to sheer chance,
then people had no control over their fates, and he
couldn't imagine anything he'd like less.

"Maybe it's the same thing," she countered. "If
you didn't go to the gallery, then we would never have
met, and I would not be having the best hamburger I
have ever had."

That was all true. But their meeting had its roots
in something very calculated, not happenstance,
which he suddenly couldn't seem to forget. Honesty

was a part of his makeup, and it didn't sit well to be so far on the wrong side of it with Claire.

He shifted uncomfortably in his seat, wondering if now was the right time to spill everything. But then she leaned in, and things got very close, very fast.

"Can I ask you something really serious?" she asked.

"Yeah."

At this point, he half expected her to ask if she thought the way they'd met had some mystical resonance to it, which he'd have a difficult time answering honestly when the answer was a resounding no. But he'd tell her the truth if she did ask. No matter the consequences.

"Can we order more French fries?" she asked instead with a gleam in her eye that made him laugh.

"Only if we also get another chocolate shake."

So he'd skated through another possible pitfall. Eventually he wouldn't be so lucky, and the secret he was carrying around would come out. He wanted it to. It was the only way to move forward with her, which had been the whole point of this casual second date—to see if there was something here worth pursuing.

There was.

"That sounds like a plan," she said with a captivating smile.

"Yes."

He lifted a finger toward the waitress and pointed at the fries, then drew a circle in the air to indicate another round. She nodded her understanding, which meant he didn't have to interrupt this illuminating conversation with Claire.

He hadn't been kidding when he'd told Helen that he liked Claire, and spending more time with her hadn't changed that.

"I've got to say I'm having a really good time with you, Doctor," she murmured.

Clearly, she'd arrived at the same conclusion. Which made him smile on the inside as much as the outside.

"I've got to say I'm having a really good time with you, Chef. What are you doing on Friday night?"

"I don't know. What am I doing?"

Good answer. They shared a long, charged look that did more to energize him than a three-mile run through light drizzle, his favorite way to exercise.

Looked like he and Claire would be moving on to the third date—a record for him lately. And he had a feeling that if things continued on this path, he'd quickly lose track of the number of dates he'd had with Claire. He couldn't find a thing wrong with that.

Except for the part where she didn't know the real truth about how they'd met.

Eleven

"WE GOT IT!"

Marco tore into the kitchen, his reading glasses perched on his nose, a dead giveaway that he'd been reading something on his phone.

"We got what?" Claire levered a spatula under another cinnamon roll and transferred it to the platter that would sit on the second shelf of the case out front.

"Unofficial, unconfirmed." Her partner threw up a hand in additional warning, as if the verbal part might not be enough to temper whatever he was about to say, and rounded the silver work area to hold his phone out toward Claire. "But I just got a tip that the Wandering Gourmet is coming here."

It took less than point four seconds for Claire to process the enormity of Marco's statement. Spatula forgotten, she stared at him as infectious smiles spread over both of their faces.

"We're going to get a review," she breathed.

Gilded Sweets Bakery was going to *get a review*.

Claire had met Eric, her mother had backed off,

and her pastries would be the talk of town. It was true what they said about good things happening in threes.

"Hopefully. Probably," he amended as he took off his glasses, his dark eyes gleaming. It was so cute how he was turning positive right before her eyes. "Here's the thing. You never know when. You don't even know what the guy looks like. He could bust you or he could praise you, and you'd never even know he was here."

These were valid points. That was when the panic set in.

"Okay, we need to change our menu."

The whole thing was completely wrong for a surprise assessment of the bakery. They had to put fancier offerings out there, dishes that called for rarer ingredients. Maybe keep some of the same, but rename the items according to a theme.

As she started to suggest that Marco could come up with cute names for his bread, he shook his head.

"No, we just need to pack the place with satisfied customers. And maybe your boyfriend can bring in some of his friends."

That tore Claire right out of the menu-palooza going on in her head. "He's not my boyfriend. We're just dating."

"Did you tell your mother about it?"

The look on Marco's face piled guilt on top of guilt.

"No! No," she said a little more quietly and without the screech the second time. "As soon as I say I like a guy, she starts naming her grandkids."

Eric was still new and still perfect. It'd be a shame to ruin that with reality. Particularly the kind that made Claire start thinking about next steps, which she did not want to do. Not yet. She'd rushed into a relationship in the past, and it still stung how quickly that had gone south.

And she shouldn't be worried about that right now. That was what happened when Helen got in the middle of things. Who could blame Claire for keeping such an important secret?

"Okay," Marco said, though his tone indicated it was anything but okay. "You know how she feels when you keep her in the dark."

"I do. I know that. We're actually having lunch today, and I'm sure she's going to grill me, per usual." And that was more than enough about that. Claire took the extra plate of cinnamon rolls into the cooler, though the way things had been going, it'd end up in the case out front sooner rather than later. "We're going to get a review!"

The screech was back, but she didn't care.

"Yes!" Marco called after her.

"We're going to get a review!" It bore repeating. And it was a far better thing to focus on than Eric. The menu, she could control. Everything else was up to fate.

"We need more customers," Marco muttered, likewise off in his own thoughts.

The cooler did nothing to cool Claire's sudden fervor. She had so much to do and who knew how long to do it. That was the problem with an anonymous reviewer who could make or break Gilded Sweets—the element of surprise.

Good thing Claire had a lot of practice working with whatever destiny dropped in her lap.

Sam Michaels had always been the man with a plan, and taking his wife on a trip to Italy—before they were both too old to enjoy it—was no exception. The problem seemed to be that Helen didn't want to follow the plan.

For the first time in thirty-plus years, their marriage had started floundering. He had no clue what to do about it. Digging into the Italy plan wasn't working. But he had no plan B.

Things had gotten a little...strained around the house. So much so, that Sam had invited his brother over for lunch to ease things. But the moment Arnie walked through the door, he'd asked about Italy. His brother wanted to take his wife on a similar trip for their anniversary, and he'd been grilling Sam on the details.

As had been the case for nearly two weeks now, when Sam mentioned the word "Italy," his lovely, enigmatic wife turned into a giant popsicle and froze him out.

Helen was currently in the kitchen, taking her sweet time fetching rolls from the oven so she didn't have to take part in the conversation, he was pretty sure.

"When are you guys leaving?" Arnie asked and handed back the tour company brochure Sam had paged through so many times, it had started to fall apart at the creases.

"As soon as *amore mio* picks a date," he said as Helen brought a platter to the table. He glanced up at her, and words fell out of his mouth. "You know, if we don't get tickets soon, our whole itinerary gets scrapped."

Now why had he said that? He knew better by now than to push her on this trip. It had gotten him nowhere thus far, and had maybe even caused a little damage in the process.

But if they didn't get to Capri by the end of August, they could most likely kiss the possibility of seeing the Blue Grotto *arrivederci*. In September, the rainy season started and the water level sometimes rose so high that boats couldn't get through the entrance to the cave. It was a gamble he wasn't willing to take. What was the point of going to Italy if you couldn't see all the things you'd planned?

"We're eating our way across Italy," Helen told Arnie, her tone laced with the sarcasm that had no place in a conversation about the dream trip they'd been talking about for years.

"You two are such foodies," Arnie said affectionately as Helen used tongs to transfer a roll to his full plate.

"We'll probably gain fifty pounds," she said, sitting down with her own plate.

Sam couldn't help it. He had to ask. "Is there any part of this trip that you like?"

Helen gave him a withering look that spoke volumes. None of which he wanted to hear.

Seeming to sense the tension, Arnie laughed half-heartedly. "I could think of worse ways to spend my old age."

"Old age." She pointed at her brother-in-law and glanced at Sam with a dawning look of horror. "My point exactly. I feel like we're packing it in."

Packing *up* and taking each other to a place drenched in romance and fine wine and food. It was a chance to reconnect—which their marriage sorely needed. If only Helen felt that way, things would be golden. But she didn't even seem to care that he missed her and wanted to spend time with her…*without* having to compete with her job and her obsessive need to interfere in Claire's life.

Speaking of which, their daughter finally rolled through the door, calling out "Hey!" as she shut it behind her.

"Hey," Sam repeated and shoveled food in his mouth.

It was a lame attempt to avoid the subject of Italy, but he'd run out of ways to stop arguing with Helen about something that should've been effortless. To say he was bewildered and unbalanced would be an understatement. For the first time in their marriage, he didn't know what to say to his wife.

"Sorry I'm late," Claire said and set a bag of goodies from the bakery on the counter in the kitchen.

"Marco and I are redoing the entire menu for this phantom reviewer. He'd better show up."

"Well, your tiramisu is the best on the planet," Helen said with love, her support for Claire always in the forefront.

Claire washed her hands in the double sink as Helen offered Sam a second roll. Which he took, because they only had rolls once a week due to the strict carb limitations Helen had put him on once he'd turned fifty. In Italy, he'd use the trip as an excuse to eat whatever he wanted.

"Yes," Claire said. "A tiny bit over the top, but I appreciate the sentiment."

"Well, hang in there, honey," he told her. "Every new business is slow to take off."

Both Sam and Helen made it a point to encourage Claire, who'd had a rough time starting up the bakery. Helen dropped by Gilded Sweets three or four times a week, and lately Sam had begun to wonder if Claire wasn't part of the reason he and Helen had started drifting apart. They'd only had the one kid, a shock to them both since they'd planned to have more, but life didn't always give you exactly what you wanted. So they'd doted on their only daughter.

Helen took it to the extreme, though, and poked her nose in Claire's business far too often. If Sam wasn't competing with Helen's clients for her attention, he was constantly rescheduling things because his wife took off on an impromptu shopping trip with their daughter. It was almost like she preferred doing anything that didn't involve him.

His wife was slipping away, and he felt powerless to stop it.

"Mushroom risotto?" Helen asked as Claire slid into a seat next to Arnie.

"Just a little bit," Claire said. "It smells so good. I have to get back to work."

Sam refrained from pointing out that she'd just arrived. Claire rarely had a lot of free time, which was why Sam tried to be patient about the time Helen spent with her. Running a bakery demanded a lot of Claire, and they had to fit around her schedule, not the other way around.

"How's my favorite niece?" Arnie asked.

"Oh, I am—I'm fine, Uncle Arnie. Thank you." Claire took the dish of risotto from Helen, clearly distracted.

"Jill tells me you met a nice fellow," Arnie said.

You could've heard a hair hit the floor as all eyes shifted to Claire, his included. This was news to him. And Helen too, apparently, or he'd know. Wouldn't he? Or was Helen keeping this kind of stuff close to the vest all of a sudden?

Claire's expression froze as she stared at her mother with a somewhat pained smile. "That's what I wanted to talk to you about. It's really new, so don't get too excited."

Ha. That was like telling Wall Street not to get too excited when a private company with a billion-dollar valuation decided to do an initial public offering of their stock.

"Does new guy have a name?" Sam asked before his wife could erupt like Mount St. Helens.

"Yes," Claire said. "Doctor Eric Carlton."

"A doctor," Helen repeated with a calm that didn't go with the subject at hand. "What field of medicine?"

"He's a pediatrician," Claire responded dutifully, which pleased Helen to no end, Sam could tell.

"Well, I like David or Diane for your firstborn," Helen said with complete sincerity.

Which was something only his wife could pull off.

"That joke never gets old."

"Well, maybe it's not a joke this time," Helen insisted. That was how she said something so ludicrous with a straight face. She'd love it if Claire engaged with her suggestions for how to name her yet-to-be-conceived grandchildren.

Claire, as usual, rolled her eyes, clearly annoyed by the whole subject. "I barely know him."

"Well, what you know you like. Right?" Helen asked in what was clearly a rhetorical question.

It was all so simple in Helen's world. You saw something you wanted, you went after it. She was a go-getter, never-let-the-grass-grow-under-her-feet type, which he'd always considered her best quality. He'd somehow never realized it would also be the reason she'd balk at retirement.

Because that was the problem in a nutshell. She didn't like sitting around quietly, content to let the world pass her by. She had to be in the middle of things, orchestrating. Always.

If he'd realized it sooner, he might not have worked

so hard to transition his own clients to Richard, his partner at the financial advice firm they'd run together for the last fifteen years. Now he had nothing. No trip, no clients, and no wife to keep him company. Just long, lonely days ahead watching Helen ramp up her real estate business instead of winding it down.

Unless he could somehow figure out how to turn things around in their marriage. He had to. There was no other choice.

"Mom, take it easy. You haven't even met him, and you're meddling," Claire said with a hard slash of her hands meant to indicate Helen needed to back off.

Outwardly, Helen acted like she was fine with Claire's mandate. Sam was probably the only one who heard her tiny sigh.

"You're right," Helen said agreeably, to her credit. "It if works out, fine. If not, then no big deal. More risotto, anyone?"

Arnie stuck his plate out, probably to ease the tension, which may or may not have worked. Sam was the last person who could read his wife's thoughts lately.

Claire eyed her mother over her water glass. "That's way too matter-of-fact."

"Over-the-top or matter-of-fact?" Helen asked with exasperation as she spooned risotto onto Arnie's plate. "Which do you prefer?"

"Something in between would be nice."

"Fine." Helen folded her hands neatly by her plate instead of picking up her fork again. "Name your firstborn whatever you please."

For some reason, that seemed to have put her back on even footing with Claire, who smiled. "All right."

If only sorting out the Italy trip and what the lack thereof meant to his marriage would turn out to be as easily navigated.

Twelve

WHEN ERIC HAD ASKED NATE to take twenty minutes for lunch, he hadn't really intended to launch into a long spiel about Claire as they walked back to the hospital from the deli on the corner. But Nate had asked. And then mentioned how sorry he was that he'd asked. Many times.

That didn't seem to stop Eric's intense need to hash out all the things at war inside him. Namely how much he liked Claire and how terrible it was that they'd started their relationship on the wrong foot. Because he was still lying to her.

"She's also really good with kids," Eric repeated, a fact about Claire that had become a sort of mantra.

"Right, because she gave your patient a cookie."

Eric fought the urge to smack Nate, who considered sarcasm an Olympic-caliber event and practiced diligently whenever possible.

He watched a lady take the hand of her little boy so they could cross the street, thinking how simple life was for kids. That was why he enjoyed them so much. They rarely filtered themselves.

"Okay, it's just I don't know how to get around this problem with her mother," Eric confessed.

It was a killer. Not only did he have the very real issue of Helen's possible—probable—ongoing interference in Claire's life, which would affect him as well, he and Claire's mom had cooked up a scheme the woman he was dating didn't know about.

These were very real issues.

"I don't think you can," Nate said with a laugh. "That woman is obsessed."

"You're probably right. It's just...I really like this girl, Nate."

And he wished he could go back in time and meet her some other way. A way that had its roots in honesty. At least then, he and Claire could be on the same side when it came to dealing with her mother's obsessive qualities.

Right now, he was on the side with Helen. That really didn't sit well. It made him as complicit as Claire's mom, and worse, Claire didn't have a long history to draw from in order to find forgiveness when it came to Eric. She did with her mom.

"Are you sure you don't just like the pastries?" Nate mused, sticking one finger on his chin comically.

"Pretty sure." Though Claire's skills with dessert did count as a point in her favor. "I just really think there's something between us that could turn into more."

Saying it out loud made it real. He was in deep with Claire after only two dates, both of which he'd tried to keep as casual as possible. So they wouldn't mean anything.

That was the problem when talking about someone as special as her. They could hang out at a dog grooming place, and it would mean something.

"Careful. The carbs are clouding your judgment."

Nate's warning might be meant in jest, but Eric took it seriously. He was letting the circumstances get away from him, and at his core, he believed he was still a good guy, the kind who always did the right thing even when it got hard.

One more date. The third one. If it went well, he'd tell her everything.

Marco and Claire stood behind the counter neurotically analyzing each customer, as had become their habit lately. At least it had gotten them both out of the kitchen and in front of customers. Usually, they were both buried in flour and didn't see the light of day for weeks on end.

It was just that the Wandering Gourmet review could make their bakery the happening spot in the Lake Union district. Maybe even all of Seattle. Claire would take either one. But to get there, they had to impress this mystery guest without benefit of forewarning.

Which they would. They were on the cusp of greatness. She could feel it. They'd put in the hard work, and it was time to reap the benefits.

"That guy right there," Marco whispered hotly and pointed at the hipster in the corner, who was definitely glancing around with a slightly narrowed gaze, as if he was taking in the ambience. "That could be him with his designer glasses."

Could be. Except another hipster guy came in and joined him, sliding into the opposite seat at the white table.

"He's meeting somebody," Claire said, which didn't necessarily rule him out. But it didn't seem likely that a critic would do a review while hanging out with a friend.

The door chime jangled as someone new came in. Which gave Marco brand-new fodder.

"Oh, look at this guy—he's definitely a critic," he murmured. "He's so judgmental."

How did you arrive at the conclusion that someone was judgmental? All the guy had done was look at his watch. And a second later, a woman pushing a baby carriage approached him, whom he swept into a long hug.

"A critic who's meeting his wife and baby? I don't think so." Claire's gaze roved over the crowd and rested on a lone woman at the long butcher block counter along the east wall. "What about her?"

The Wandering Gourmet could be a woman. There were no rules.

Besides, the dark-haired woman had been chatting with Danielle, their part-time waitress, for several minutes. Grilling her about the menu's ingredients? Asking where the ingredients originated?

"Claire, she comes in every morning like clock-work," Marco told her. "Double macchiato and a blueberry scone."

Gilded Sweets had *regulars?* She might need to sit down for a minute. "Wow."

That was... She didn't know what that was. Fantastic, sure. A milestone. She and Marco exchanged glances as the enormity of it washed over her. People came into the bakery on a regular basis because they liked it the *best* of all the places around.

Claire definitely needed to come out of the kitchen on a lot more frequent basis.

A young man wearing dark blue scrubs approached the counter, his smile bright and his carriage animated.

"The food was great," he told them, raising his voice and calling over his shoulder. "I especially enjoyed the olive bread."

Another of Eric's friends sent over from the hospital, most likely, and apparently he'd been instructed to make a big hoopla while he was at it.

"Thank you," Marco said, his smile a little misty, because a compliment for his bread was a compliment, no matter how it had been solicited.

"I really do enjoy the food," the young man murmured on the down-low.

And that made Claire smile. "Thank you for coming."

The guy shot them a thumbs up and bounced out the door.

Marco jerked his head toward the departing medical professional. "Maybe he's the phantom critic."

And Claire had wasted enough time today evaluating customers who were paying her bills and had probably never even heard of the Wandering Gourmet. She dismissed the idea with a snort and went back to her glace.

Shrugging, Marco called after her. "Could be."

Doubtful. Besides, it didn't matter if they correctly identified the critic. Whatever happened would happen, and they had no control over it. Fate would be kind to them, though. It had worked out things in their favor so far, hadn't it?

A surprise catering job had come up for Saturday, so instead of going out with Eric on Friday night as she'd planned, Claire ended up in the kitchen at Gilded Sweets. The other surprise had been when Eric had insisted on hanging out with her. While she baked. It was the most ridiculous, wonderful thing ever, and she couldn't stop smiling.

She glanced over her shoulder, thoroughly distracted by the sight of Eric sitting at the long silver prep table, sipping the tea she'd made him. It did something fluttery to her insides to have him here in her private domain, the place she'd only ever shared with her mother and Marco.

The kitchen had tons of great memories, and she had the strongest feeling that tonight would add a few more. The thought put a tremor in her hands, and one of the decorative chocolate circles she'd been trying to set into the frosting broke. That never happened.

"By the way," she said, mostly to break the tension. "Thank you for sending all your friends in. It was very sweet."

If his campaign to increase her business had been designed as a way to her heart, he was doing a great job. The thought made the flutters kick up something fierce.

She had to get her wits about her, or this entire catering job would go south. At least she didn't have to throw away her hard work. She handed Eric the broken pieces of chocolate.

"Thank you," he said sincerely, which did nothing to quell the flutters.

She turned back to her work, determined to get it done and done right with no more broken pieces. "So your family, do they live here too?"

"Connecticut, or I would have sent them as well, I promise."

"Is that where you grew up?"

"Yup, Stanford, Connecticut since I was three years old. It's where my dad did his residency. He was a cardiologist."

"Hmm," she said noncommittally as she set another piece of chocolate into the frosting of the small cakes she hoped would be the hit of the party tomorrow.

It was hard to concentrate with so much Eric going on. His voice was amazing, so rich and textured. She could listen to him talk for hours.

"It seemed like a future in medicine was inevitable," he continued. "How about your dad?"

She really loved being able to connect with Eric while still doing her thing here at Gilded Sweets. There was a part of her that questioned whether she had time to get into a new relationship right now. Like maybe she shouldn't be trying to split her attention when the catering gig that was supposed to be a side job had suddenly exploded, and the Wandering Gourmet could waltz through the front door at any given moment.

But fate had other ideas. It felt wrong to ignore such an obvious sign from the universe. This thing had been gifted to her at this moment in her life for a reason, and besides, she really liked Eric. She thought the feeling was mutual. Tonight might be a great proving ground on that front.

She considered his question about her dad as she set another piece of chocolate.

"He's a financial advisor, but he and my mom are newly retired and about to travel to Italy together."

She could easily stop there, but Eric always listened to everything she said so attentively, as if there wasn't anything in the world more important than whatever she was about to say next. A lot of guys constantly checked their phones, even while on a date, which really annoyed her. Eric never did that, and as a pediatrician, he had the best excuse for it.

His laser focus on her hadn't shifted an iota since

he'd arrived. It felt like a good time to share the reason she thought the way her parents had met was so romantic. Why she'd held out for her own story.

"They actually met in a college bookstore," she told him. "There was one copy of *A Room with a View*, which is set in Italy, and they both needed it for an exam, so they shared it, and by the end of the book they were in love."

"Huh, that's a great story."

Yes. And the fact that he thought so spoke volumes. Enough that she couldn't help but take a tiny break from her chocolate to focus on him for a few minutes. She settled onto a stool next to him. It wasn't a hardship in the least to drink him in. He really was gorgeous with his dark hair and chiseled features that were so distinctive.

"Just think. If the clerk had more copies, I wouldn't be here."

"I think you should track down that clerk and give her a box of your pastries. It's the least you can do."

She laughed at yet another example of his blind support for her culinary skills. It really turned her head in the best way. "Okay, I'll get right on that."

One thing about Eric's laser focus: it was impossible to miss the way he was looking at her, as if he'd spotted his favorite treat inside the bakery case. It tripped her pulse and, suddenly self-conscious, she glanced away.

"I must look a mess," she announced unnecessarily, because clearly he could see that for himself. "I usually wear half of what I bake."

Served her right for choosing this instead of a real date at a nice restaurant where she didn't have to do any of the cooking. But it had been this or nothing. And she wasn't sorry at all as Eric leaned in to capture her gaze in his, refusing to let go.

The long, charged moment dragged out, impossibly thick with possibilities.

"I think you look perfect," he murmured.

Nerves kicked up a storm in her stomach as his gaze dropped to her mouth. Was he thinking about kissing? Because she sure was.

She had no idea what to say next, so she blurted out the first thing that came to mind. "Did I ever tell you when I was five, I had my first éclair? The waiter was French. I kept thinking he said 'Claire.'"

Eric took her hand, leaning even closer, intent written all over his face. He did want to kiss her, but she was still babbling about éclairs. Knowing that didn't seem to give her any special ability to stop babbling though.

"So I thought he named the dessert after me. Isn't that hilarious?"

"Hilarious," he repeated softly.

And then suddenly the words died in her throat as his mouth settled on hers. Tentatively at first, as if gauging whether she'd welcome this, but when she melted into it, he lifted a hand to her face, deepening the kiss. Eric kissed her with that same laser focus, as if there was nothing else in the world that could compare with this experience and he wanted to savor every second.

She felt the same. This was better than éclairs, better than any of the finest chocolate in the world. If the Wandering Gourmet himself walked into her bakery, she'd tell him to wait.

She was busy.

Fate had gotten the timing exactly right. This was meant to be. How many other guys would have so graciously veered from course when she'd announced she couldn't make their date?

That alone had tipped the scales. No doubt about it. She was falling for him.

Thirteen

WHEN HELEN ANSWERED HER PHONE as she was walking out the door to her first showing of the day, the very last person's voice she expected to hear was Eric's.

"Helen, we have to talk."

"Oh, hello," she said, her voice naturally rising in surprise. Glancing behind her at Sam, she casually walked out of the bedroom, where he stood fastening his watch to his wrist, praying he wouldn't follow her. "What a nice surprise."

"I need to see you right away."

"Um, sure. Is there something wrong?"

"Yeah," he said. "We have a problem."

A whole litany of possibilities scrolled through her head, and she didn't like any of them. Obviously, something had happened with Claire. Her daughter had probably told him they couldn't see each other anymore because she was too busy with the bakery. If so, she'd have a long talking-to with Claire immediately.

Huddled up in the little alcove near the stairs, Helen

whispered into the phone. "What? I thought everything was going so well?"

"Yeah," he said wryly. "That's the problem."

Sam chose that moment to head out of the bedroom and toward the stairs. She couldn't tip him off that she was talking to her daughter's boyfriend. Sam wouldn't appreciate her interference, and besides, he might tell Claire. This situation would not be improved if things got out of control.

"Uh, perhaps I could show you the house after you get off work," she said loudly, praying Eric would understand her odd segue.

Sam paused on the landing to stare at her. *Ugh.* What had she said that had gotten his attention?

"Is Claire there?" Eric asked.

She rolled her eyes. Both men clearly had no idea how to let things go.

"Not exactly," she hedged. To the hulking man on the stairs, she said, "I'll be done in just a minute, Sam."

Instead of going away like any normal person, Sam stood there listening to her conversation.

"Your husband?" Eric asked.

"Right."

"Can you meet at the Chameleon?" he suggested.

"Seven o'clock would be just fine. Bye."

She hung up before this conversation got completely out of hand. But as she put her phone to sleep, Sam scowled in her general direction.

"I thought we were going out to dinner," he said, his frustration evident.

Drat—she'd forgotten all about that. "It's just a quick showing. It shouldn't take long. I'll meet you at the restaurant."

It wasn't like she could cancel on Eric. Whatever was going on, she had to manage it. Claire could not lose this one. He was too perfect, and Helen had already done so much to help secure this relationship for her daughter. Sam would have to understand.

Besides, they'd gone out to dinner together a thousand times. There was nothing special about tonight that Sam couldn't wait for her.

But he turned and went downstairs without another word, his expression crestfallen as if she'd kicked his puppy or something. Honestly.

She fretted about the seven o'clock meeting all day and wished she could've met Eric during the day sometime, but her own idiocy with acting like she'd been talking to a client had caused it to unfold like it had. So she had no one else to blame for having to wait but herself.

Finally, the hour arrived, and she jetted into the Chameleon to find Eric already at the bar.

"Hey," she said as she touched his shoulder to alert him to her presence. "What's going on?"

"I think I'm falling for your daughter," he told her earnestly.

Relief flooded Helen's chest as she turned to slide into the next barstool. That was the big emergency? "And this is a problem because…?"

"Because every time she talks about you and how

she and I met, I have to lie. She thinks it was fate that brought us together."

The problem started to clarify. "And it was her mother."

"We need to tell her the truth."

Well, she couldn't very well argue with him. Her daughter's boyfriend had an honest streak. It spoke very highly of him, which was a point in Helen's favor. Somehow she didn't think Claire would appreciate it much.

"Okay," she said. "But please let me do it. Otherwise, she'll never forgive me."

Eric leaned in a bit, increasing the intensity of the conversation. "You have to do it soon. Because the longer you wait, the bigger the lie becomes, and neither of us are going to be able to save this relationship."

Which would be a shame. This was meant to be; she could feel it. Surely Claire wouldn't be that upset. Right? Except, Helen had all these flashbacks of Claire telling her to stay out of her love life, and she wasn't all that sure Claire would actually speak to her again once she knew the truth about Eric.

How had the simple act of telling Eric to breeze by the gallery event Claire had catered turned out to be so complicated?

Claire wandered out of the cooler, barely pausing long enough to close the door properly. All her attention was on her tablet, where she'd been reading the Wandering Gourmet's article in the new edition of Seattle Monthly.

"Ugh," she said to the screen with a scowl and then glanced up at Marco as she came into the kitchen, waited until he slid a pan of bread into the oven, and then told him, "Wow. The Wandering Gourmet does not pull any punches."

She grabbed a stool so she could sit down at the long prep table, the same one she'd sat at with Eric the other night. Where he'd kissed her, the memory of which had been giving her warm tingles all day. Until she'd opened up this issue of Seattle Monthly. She'd crashed back to earth in a hurry all right.

"Listen to this scathing review for Etoiles De Danse." She stabbed the tablet. "'I had the misfortune of ordering the Trout Almondine, which was dry as a bone.'"

Marco peered over her shoulder, his expression grave. "Oh, no. I know the chef over there. Poor guy."

"It gets worse." She read from the screen. "'The *foie gras* was as forgettable as the ambience. Cold, bland, no panache.' What if this backfires, Marco?"

Claire dropped the tablet and scrubbed at her face with both hands as the implications washed over her. The Wandering Gourmet could put them out of business. And she didn't want to think like that. It was her job to be the positive one. If she went around spewing doom and gloom, what would Marco bring to their partnership?

Okay, this wasn't like her. She had to get it together, for both of their sakes. This was what she got for letting Eric take over her every waking thought—no brain cells left for what was really important. Gilded Sweets Bakery. Her livelihood, and Marco's, depended on this review from the Wandering Gourmet.

She slid from the stool and paced around, her thoughts a whirl.

"What if we do something about the lighting?" she suggested as she pictured how much more ambience a simple change like that could bring. "Or some fresh flowers? A little linen?"

It could work.

Marco shot her a look. "I'm having nightmares wondering if this guy is going to show up and ruin our lives."

"Or save us," Claire shot back, because it was all so clear to her in that moment. "One positive review from this guy could change everything."

That was what she had to focus on. The things she could control. Fate would take care of the rest, like it always had. What was she worried about?

"Well, we're hanging on by a very thin thread here," Marco said.

"I say we give the restaurant a makeover. Before he gets here."

Now she was cooking. Not literally. That part wasn't going to be an issue, not after she and Marco had completely redone the menu. But she'd missed the ambience piece of the pie, so to speak, and thank goodness fate had gifted her with that article. It had honed her thoughts perfectly.

"I knew I should have become a fireman," Marco muttered as Claire's phone rang.

She glanced at the name flashing on the screen and answered. "Hi, Mom."

"Hi, sweetheart."

"I'm kind of busy. Can I call you later?"

"I really need to talk to you."

"Okay, but not now." Maybe not even later, at least not today. She had so much to do. "I need to fix up the restaurant. I have to go shopping."

"Well, I can go with you," her mother said immediately. "Shopping for what?"

"Panache."

"I'm on my way."

Her mother ended the call, and for the first time today, Claire breathed easier. If there was anyone who knew style and cultured grace, it was Helen Michaels. Claire should have thought to call her immediately, but with the Wandering Gourmet and Eric taking up all of the real estate in her brain, she'd had nothing left over to really think things through.

Of course her mother would be here for her in Claire's hour of need. She always had been before. Why would a professional crisis be any different?

Helen dropped her phone into her purse and tried to calm her racing pulse. It was now or never. Claire needed to know the truth about Eric, and what better time to tell her than during a shopping trip?

They'd bond over tablecloths, and Claire would realize how important their relationship was. Sure, she'd be a little mad that Helen had interfered again, but the end result would be worth it. Right?

She put on a light jacket in case it started drizzling and went outside to let Sam know she was leaving. He'd been out in the yard all morning spreading out endless bags of mulch he'd bought at the home improvement store.

"Claire and I are going shopping," she called to him.

Sam paused, stabbing the long shovel in his gloved hands into the ground and leaning on it as he stared at her. "I thought we were going to see the travel agent today."

The look on his face cut through her. She'd genuinely forgotten that. Mostly because she hadn't really intended to go in the first place. "Oh, maybe later."

They had plenty of time to plan this trip. Italy wasn't going anywhere. He'd said that himself, hadn't he? Or had he been blowing smoke in hopes that she'd cave sooner rather than later, giving in to the idea of retirement without so much as a whimper?

"Later?" he repeated in that voice that tried and convicted her with no room for her to plead her case. Later was obviously *not fine*.

"Don't be like that. Claire needs me."

Surely he understood that. Claire came first. Always.

"She's a grown woman. She can shop alone."

Well, yes, of course. But what was the point of

that? Shopping alone sounded as appealing as dying alone. And retiring was one step closer to *that*, so no thank you.

Besides, it wasn't like she could come right out and tell Sam that Eric had given her an ultimatum. That she had to talk to Claire before everything Helen had worked for fell apart.

"It's not just that. She and I need to have a talk," Helen explained.

"About what?"

"This doctor she's been seeing—"

He groaned without even letting her finish. "Oh, Helen. Don't start interfering again."

"It's just a little girl talk," she corrected hastily. "My interfering days are over. That's what I wanted to tell her."

She was turning over a new leaf. Maybe once Claire got settled with Eric, then Helen could think about the rest of her life. Taking it slower at her real estate agency. Going to Italy for a few weeks instead of a few months. It might be fun, as long as she could talk Claire and Eric into having a long engagement so Helen didn't miss any of the wedding planning.

"She knows that you love her," Sam called as Helen scurried to the car. "That's all that matters."

That and Helen's ability to get people together. Her track record had no parallel. She couldn't let this thing between Claire and Eric get out of hand before he had a chance to propose.

Oh, my. What if they wanted to get married right

away? She couldn't be in *Italy* while Claire picked out her wedding dress by herself. It was unfathomable.

No Italy. Not for a while. Sam would have to understand.

She and Claire tried a store they'd never been to before. It was closer to Pike Place than Helen would have liked, due to all the tourist traffic. But the small shop had a markedly smaller crowd than she'd anticipated, making it easier to pick out some great things for Gilded Sweets.

The moment Helen stepped over the threshold, she beelined it for a pale gold tray, picking it up to show Claire. "This would be great for serving pastries."

"Oh." Her daughter glanced it with a critical eye and gave a half shrug. "Get two. They're half off. Look at this tablecloth."

Claire wandered over to the display and fingered the fabric with a little sigh when she spied the price, which must be out of budget.

"That's nice," Helen said and figured Claire needed a distraction from overpriced tablecloths. No time like the present to get the elephant out of the room. "Um… Listen, I wanted to talk to you about something, darling."

"About what?"

"This doctor you've been dating—"

"Eric."

The man's name left her mouth in a rush as if she'd shut it up inside her and had been waiting for Helen to ask so she could let out all the things at once. A glow took over her whole face as she set down the salt and pepper shaker set in her hand.

"You're going to love him," Claire continued, her voice threaded with something Helen had never heard before—giddiness.

Over a man. It was so highly unusual that Helen could only stare as Claire wandered off in a blissful daze, still spouting at the mouth about Eric.

"He's kind, he's honest. I really feel like he's someone I can trust."

Helen hid a wince. Great. That was a fabulous quality in a potential mate. Too bad she was about to stomp all over that one.

"And did I mention he is gorgeous?" Claire gushed in what was literally the first time her daughter had used that tone in relation to something other than a pastry. "It was just so romantic the way we met. It was kind of like you and Dad. There's all these people in the gallery, and somehow we...found each other. Clearly we were meant to meet."

Spear, right to the heart. This was an unmitigated disaster of the highest order, and Eric had been so very right to call her. Claire had latched onto how she'd met Eric as some kind of sign from the universe, when all along, the truth lurked beneath the surface of this new relationship, a truth that would ruin everything.

Helen knew these things. She could sense them. And Claire wasn't going to take the news of her mother's interferences well at all.

She opened her mouth. And closed it. Stared at

the floor in hopes a miracle would somehow appear right there on the hardwood planks to save her from this impossible quandary.

"Oh, they're practically giving these away," Claire told her brightly, oblivious to the churn in Helen's stomach, and held up a vase with a cutout pattern that would be lovely with a candle inside. "What about one of these on each table with an arrangement?"

Of flowers? No. With those cutouts, that vase was made for candlelight, which would throw all these romantic shadows on the table—which was none of Helen's concern. She was out of the romance business, and rightly so.

Hadn't she made enough of a mess of things?

"Maybe not?" Claire prompted. "What do you think?"

"What do I think?" Helen shook her head. "I think from now on, you should just make all your own choices."

"Just asking about the vase," Claire called as Helen pretended to be interested in a display of hanging pots. "Aside from my love life, I really value your opinion, Mom."

Fine. Then Gilded Sweets needed these half-off trays. She yanked one from its display and tucked it under her arm with a forced smile.

How was she going to tell Claire the truth about Eric? Her daughter would be crushed. And her relationship with Eric would be affected, maybe permanently, as might the one between mother and daughter. Besides, did Claire need an extra burden right now with her angst over Gilded Sweets and this gourmet review? It was all she'd talked about on the car ride over.

No, the timing was wrong. All at once, she couldn't do it. It was too much to risk.

Fourteen

I F ERIC KEPT UP THIS pacing, he'd wear a hole in the carpet. Fortunately, Nate had found a way to stand right in his path about eleven billion times and also stretch out the job of making copies to take fifteen minutes. Being in the wrong place at the wrong time was a gift, one Nate relished.

"Helen is calling Claire now," Eric told Nate without being asked, mostly because Nate was his friend at the end of the day.

And he needed someone to talk him off the ledge. Which ledge, he wasn't sure. All he knew was that his skin felt like it had been doused in gasoline and set on fire. He couldn't stay still.

What if this secret coming out ruined everything?

"Wow, it's a little late in the game for that, don't you think?" Nate asked.

When Nate didn't have a snarky comeback for something going on in Eric's life, it was bad.

"Maybe." Late wasn't the same as too late, right? Eric paused in his pacing, compelled to explain himself. "I mean, I wanted to tell her myself, but Helen insisted that she tell Claire."

Donna breezed by. "That's right. You can't come between a mother and her daughter."

"That's right." Eric smiled at her with relief. *Thank you, Donna, for making my point.*

Claire would feel the same way. She had to. There was no reason to be so antsy.

But his legs had a mind of their own, eating up the carpet as they took him on another tour of the hallway.

"I just wonder why she's not calling," Eric wondered and then realized he'd said it out loud. Like a big dork.

"Who?" Donna asked. "Helen or Claire?"

"To be honest," Eric said, "at this point, I'd take a call from either one."

There was something really wrong about the fact that Eric's office staff knew his girlfriend's mother enough to call her by name and Claire had no idea. Or a clue that Helen and Eric had each other's phone numbers. That they'd had coffee together. Had hung out at the Chameleon together. Twice.

It was way past time to get this all out in the open.

"Well, look at it this way," Nate threw in helpfully. "If it doesn't pan out with Claire, the lovely Doctor Dana Becker is still waiting in the wings. I ran into her in the elevator. She asked about you."

Dana. That was a name he hadn't thought about in a while. But there was no spark there. Dating Dana again after Claire would be like someone handing you gelatin after you'd eaten one bite of the most exquisite mocha truffle cheesecake.

Look at him with the dessert metaphors. Claire had really gotten under his skin.

Donna shot Nate a withering glance. "I think you're missing the point. He's in love with Claire."

What? No, he wasn't. It was way too soon for that.

Sure, he'd told Helen he was falling for Claire. But honestly, he'd kind of thrown that out to the woman as an excuse to get the truth on the table. Had he been speaking more from the heart than he'd realized?

"You're in love with her now?" Nate asked with a smirk. His default expression lately.

"I don't know," Eric hedged, mostly because he really didn't but also because he had zero interest in confessing a thing to his buddy, not when grief would be the likely result of that. "Look. All I know for sure is I don't want to lose her. At all. Do you think I should call her?"

Nate shook his head no at the same moment Donna murmured, "Uh-huh," and nodded with exaggeration to counter Nate.

"No," Nate said as Donna punched him in the arm.

"Yes," she insisted.

Well, that was helpful. Eric stalked back to his office to contemplate all the ways he'd screwed up the best thing that had ever happened to him.

The map of Italy that had been hanging behind Sam's desk for the last fifteen years lay on the dining room table. It was the first time he'd taken the mounted map out of its frame, but desperate times called for desperate measures.

His wife needed a little reminder of why they'd talked about going to Italy in the first place. Maybe Sam needed it, too.

They'd been at such cross purposes lately. Drifting apart. After Helen had blown off their trip to the travel agency, and then shown up late to the dinner he'd planned as a way to reconnect, he'd decided to take the bull by the horns.

He poured his wife a glass of Chianti, which she readily took, handed her the case containing her reading glasses, and parked her in the chair that had the best view of the map. She'd slipped on the glasses and hadn't bolted yet, so he took that as a good sign. He'd bought these special pins to stick in his beloved map as he let his vision of this dream trip unfold, so this was no random drive-by Italy discussion.

This was serious business.

So far, she'd managed to find any excuse not to hear the itinerary, but he'd begged her to listen to his plan in case there was something she wanted to change. If he did it right, Helen would hear all the passion in his voice for this once-in-a-lifetime opportunity to really set the tone for the second half of their lives.

"And so, *amore mio.*" Sam leaned over his wife's shoulder and stuck a pin in the little dot of pink just off the eastern Italian coast. "We start in Venice, then head south to Tuscany. *Molto romantico.*"

She responded dutifully, "*Si.*"

Which was enough encouragement to keep going. Maybe this had been the right step. It was certainly getting him excited.

"And then Pisa. Florence."

He stuck a pin in both and glanced at her, but she wasn't even listening. She chugged her wine with this look on her face he couldn't interpret. But he knew enough to realize that her attention wasn't on him. Which made his heart sink a little. Distraction. That was why she hadn't bolted.

"*Come stai?*" he asked her gently, and when she raised a brow, he translated. "How are you?"

"Don't ask."

That sounded ominous. He took his best stab at reading her mind, never an easy task. "Did everything go okay with Claire?"

"Oh, it was fine." But she took off her reading glasses, clearly done humoring him with this jaunt through his painstaking plans.

"Just…fine?" he prompted, because it didn't sound like it had gone fine.

"There was so much I wanted to say and I just couldn't find the words. Now it may be too late."

So something *was* going on with Claire. That

marked maybe the first time in recent memory that he'd correctly guessed the source of his wife's angst.

"What do you mean?"

She hesitated so long in answering that he wasn't sure she actually intended to, but then she gestured off-handedly at the map. "You know, if we go on this trip..."

"'If?'" he repeated as his heart did a little more than sink. It splatted to the floor in a big, giant mess. "What happened to 'when?'"

"Look, there's a lot on my mind, Sam. Can we just talk about this some other time?" she said with a scowl so unlike her that he genuinely had a bad moment as he collapsed into the chair at the head of the table.

It was time to call it.

"If this trip to Italy is going to make you so miserable, then let's forget it."

The words physically pained him to say. But he didn't take them back.

"That's not what I mean—"

"No," he cut in. "I just wanted to make you happy. I'm not sure I know how to do that anymore."

That was the bottom line. He'd been planning this trip for as long as he could remember. Since studying *A Room with a View*, while falling for this amazing woman he'd stumbled over in the bookstore. Somehow over the years, they'd ended up on different paths, and he'd stopped to look around for his missing companion far too late.

"If you figure it out," he told her, "let me know."

"Sam—"

"No. I'm not making any more plans."

He was done trying to force this attempt at reconnection down her throat. She clearly had no interest in the trip. Maybe she didn't even have an interest in their marriage any longer. Maybe her distraction hadn't stemmed from the shopping trip with Claire, but because she'd been trying to figure out how to tell him they were on different paths.

If so, that was not okay. *He* was not okay. With any of this.

Something had to give, and he was afraid of what that might be.

"Italy will still be there next year," he said. "It's you and me that I worry about."

And in the most telling part of this whole conversation, she didn't correct him.

Nor did she stop him as he walked out of the room.

Not only had Claire not called Eric, but when he called her, she didn't answer. After three tries, he made himself stop, because he wasn't that guy. Or at least, he'd never been that guy before.

She didn't want to talk to him. At all. Obviously.

He shouldn't call her again. Right?

When a woman picked up her phone, the very last thing she needed to see was about four hundred missed calls from the guy she was avoiding. Pathetic much? Claire might have turned him into a big mess.

Clearly his history with her mother lent credence to that possibility. The fact that he'd driven to her house and noted the lack of a red Mini Cooper in the front also proved the point.

Driving to Gilded Sweets in the rain sealed the deal, though. He was nuts.

But she *was* inside. He could barely make out Claire's form from the street as he cruised by, but what other woman would be up on a ladder messing with the lighting inside her bakery at nine o'clock at night?

There was nothing to do but knock on the glass door and hope she wasn't so angry with him that she left him standing outside like a moron. But then, it would be no less than he deserved.

He couldn't stand not knowing exactly how upset she was after finding out the deception. Mad enough to stop seeing him? Mad enough to post pictures on social media of her burning him in effigy? Or simply upset that he hadn't told her the truth about her mother's involvement in getting them together, and now that she'd had time to think about it, she might be able to forgive him if he begged hard enough?

Door number three. He hoped. Only one way to find out. He knocked.

She glanced over her shoulder with a faint smile that did all kinds of strange things to his insides. She didn't look furious. In fact...she didn't even look mad. And she immediately came over to unlock the door.

"Hi," she said. "What are you doing here?"

Since that should be obvious, he drank her in for

a second, and then stepped inside at her urging, glad she hadn't immediately torn a strip off of his hide. "I wanted to come see you."

And do whatever it took to salvage this relationship. If nothing else, this problem with the truth of how they'd gotten together had shown him how much he needed things to work out.

"Oh, well. Hello."

She shut the door and locked it again. Possibly so no one outside could testify where she'd hid his body.

"I tried calling you earlier," he said casually as if that might be news to her.

"Oh, yeah. My phone died. It probably went straight to voicemail."

Well. Then it *had* been news to her. If she hadn't bothered to charge her phone, she hadn't intended to use it to call him, that was for sure. An awkward silence fell as she sank into a chair and buried her head in her hands with a groan that said she wasn't sure what to say either.

Not on her to figure that out. This was his mess to clean up. "Yeah, so I just wanted to know how you were feeling."

He bit back the rest because she needed a chance to vent all her frustration before he fell prostrate at her feet with flowery phrases designed to convince her how truly sorry he was.

"Right now, I'm tired," she said, her face reflecting exactly that.

"I meant about us." Nothing like laying it all out there.

Confusion marred her brow line as she stared at him, clearly conflicted or something. "I don't know what you want me to say."

If that didn't put it all in perspective... "Just the truth."

Way past time for that. And from here on out, it would be nothing but the truth. As long as she forgave him, they could weather anything.

"The truth is, I'm confused."

"And you should be." What had happened with her mother had gotten all out of hand.

"Are you confused?" she asked.

A fair question. She deserved to hear the truth about how he felt, and confusion wasn't it. "No, I'm concerned."

"About what?"

Now she looked concerned, and his head was starting to spin from how quickly this conversation had gone someplace other than he'd anticipated. All at once, it occurred to him that she might not even be mad at all. Like, maybe Helen had done such a great job explaining that Eric had had zero involvement in the scheme that it had never even occurred to Claire to be upset with him. And here he was acting like a doofus about it, assuming she'd flipped out.

Starting over.

"Sorry," he said with a smile. "How was your day today?"

"*Ugh*," she said with a return half smile that did nice things to his insides. "I read a horrible review on another restaurant, so I decided to spruce this place up, and then my mom and I went shopping."

"Right. And how did that go with your mom?"

He braced himself in case he'd mistaken all of this for the lead-up to the part where she related how her mother had spilled everything, and upon reflection, Claire really was mad.

"Great!" she said brightly.

"Good. That's great." The relief in his voice couldn't be helped, and for some reason, that put a furrow across Claire's brow.

"What? My mom and I always go shopping to-gether."

"Yes, but today went really well."

"Yeah," she said. "I got a couple of tablecloths and some trays."

"Good. And you're not…not, you know, mad?"

"No, I'm not mad. They were half-price." She let that sink in, but before he could figure out if it was supposed to be a joke or not, she continued. "Oh, and I talked to my mom about you and how we met. And they want to meet you."

His smile froze as he filtered through all of the words she'd said and how they didn't go together—*if* she'd been made aware that Helen and Eric had already met. Several times. Which didn't seem to be a known fact yet.

No wonder this conversation had seemed a lot like two people reading from completely different scripts.

Claire was still gazing at him expectantly, so he had to say *something*. "That's great."

"So I was thinking maybe this weekend?"

"Fantastic."

He laughed, mostly to dispel the tension that had sprung up along the back of his neck—for no reason apparently—and that made her laugh too. Then she reached out to take his hands in hers, sealing the alternate reality that he'd fallen into.

Helen hadn't said a blessed word to Claire about the truth.

The woman had to fix this now. *Before* Claire dragged Eric to meet her parents, one of whom was still lying to her daughter.

The next morning, Eric took a break between patients to run to the dry cleaners, which gave him the perfect opportunity to call Helen.

She answered on the first ring.

"Hi, Helen, it's Eric," he said, his tone bordering on irritated. Because he was.

"I'm so sorry," she said with a weird little lilt to her voice. "I just wasn't able to close the deal."

So she wasn't even going to pretend to misunderstand. "All you did was shop."

"That's right. Thank you for understanding."

Helen might very well succeed at driving him around the bend. "I *don't* understand."

Nor would he if she didn't start telling him what she was up to.

"Of course not."

"Okay, I'm confused." An understatement. "Are you speaking cryptically or literally?"

"Exactly," she said with false cheer, which told him exactly nothing.

And she needed to start making a whole lot more sense. His relationship with Claire hung in the balance while Helen played these mind games. "We need to meet."

She seemed to do much better face to face. Which was fine. Claire was worth taking some extra time to clear this up with her mother, once and for all.

"Great. Just text me when and where. I appreciate you giving me a second chance to earn your business."

He rolled his eyes, because really? Claire's mom took the cake. And not the good kind of cake Claire baked but the crazy cake he'd apparently signed up for by letting Helen get in the middle of his relationship with her daughter. Of course, he wouldn't have met Claire otherwise...so he'd slog it out to the bitter end of this issue with Helen and move on.

He texted her directions to the park near the hospital with a time that would hopefully work for her, since it was the only space he had in a jam-packed schedule.

She'd better be there. If not, Eric would tell Claire the truth himself, whether Helen liked it or not.

Fifteen

MARCO TOOK TWO PLATES FROM Claire and jetted over to table twelve to serve the couple seated there. As he set down the hazelnut crepes and the tiramisu, a clean-cut gentleman in an expensive suit came into the bakery, clearly sizing the place up with his discerning eye.

Oh, man. This guy had Wandering Gourmet stamped all over him, as if he'd never be satisfied with anything less than perfection. His deep blue suit complimented his dark skin, and his glasses rode high on his nose as if placed there specifically to peer down at you in disdain. Even his shoes looked like they wouldn't dare pick up dirt without his permission.

Marco's eyes widened as he noticed the guy. Furtively, Marco caught Claire's gaze and pointed surreptitiously in the direction of the suit, his assessment of the man's likely identity on the same wavelength as Claire's.

As Marco joined her behind the counter, she murmured, "Do you think that's him?"

"I don't know," he whispered hotly. "Everyone's looking like a critic to me now."

Deep breath. "Okay. I got this."

She skirted Marco and grabbed a corked bottle of water, then wove through the sea of tables to fill the glass of Mr. Presumed Wandering Gourmet.

"Hello, how are you?" she asked pleasantly, thrilled beyond belief that she didn't actually sound like a woman whose heart was about to beat right out of her chest. "Today's specials are Brie en Croute with freshly baked rosemary bread. Homemade scones with raspberry glaze. And of course, our Coconut Lime Tart."

"Why *of course*?" Mr. Gourmet asked with thinly veiled confusion as he glanced up at her from behind those discerning glasses.

Ugh, what was wrong with her? Mr. Gourmet wouldn't know what Gilded Sweets prided itself on unless she told him. She was such a ding-dong. "Well, because the Coconut Lime Tart is one of our most popular items, so of course it is one of our specials."

Good. Okay. He wasn't looking at her like she'd turned into a red-footed booby before his eyes.

"Very well. I'll let you know when I've decided."

"Great." And now there was nothing left to do but walk away. Yet she wasn't walking away. "You just take your time."

Okay, now she needed to make herself scarce before she freaked him out even more with her hovering.

She dashed back to the relative safety of the area behind the counter, convinced her flaming cheeks would set fire to something if she didn't calm down. *Way to almost blow it.*

Marco lifted his brows as she passed him.

"I don't know," she muttered and kept going to somewhere she couldn't see Mr. Gourmet. Out of sight, out of mind.

Except it didn't work like that, because Marco tracked her down in the cooler—which wasn't cooling her down as expected—to throw more monkey wrenches in the gears by telling her Mr. Gourmet was ready to order.

A croissant and a scone. That was it? No Coconut Lime Tart?

Dutifully, she brought him the best of the lot and then realized. The Wandering Gourmet could even now at this moment be eating something she'd made. And evaluating it. For a review.

She couldn't resist peeking out into the dining room, but the stupid cash register blocked her view. The couple at the next table over from Mr. Gourmet got up to leave, and she used that as an excuse to scurry over to snag their dirty dishes. Couldn't have Mr. Gourmet thinking Gilded Sweets ran a sloppy ship.

She smiled at him, noting his own empty plate.

Empty!

Quick as lightning, she ran back to the kitchen, dumped the dishes, and squealed to Marco, "He ate the croissant! Every last bite. And the scone too."

He pumped his fist in the air with a little shout of triumph, a display of optimism that was becoming less rare.

"Do you think I should offer him anything else?" she asked, her lungs doing this funny thing where they didn't want to act like lungs and let her breathe.

Marco dropped off a loaf of bread on the cooling rack and turned to her in a flash, spreading his hands out in a sharp, flat line. "No, we don't want him to know that we suspect it's him. Let's just let him enjoy his coffee."

Smart. She skipped backward toward the front of the bakery, nearly tripping over her own two feet as Marco followed her. As they cleared the counter, a lady in her late thirties with short hair and a pretty medium-brown complexion dashed through the door and buzzed right up to Mr. Gourmet to drop a kiss onto his cheek.

"Who's she?" Marco asked under his breath.

"I don't know," Claire shot back. "Maybe it's part of his cover."

"Okay, go find out." Marco shooed her in the couples' direction.

Why did she have to do all of the dirty work? "No."

"Yes. Go."

She heaved a sigh. But really, this train had already left the station. Might as well hop aboard. Or something like that.

She approached the table with as good of a smile as she could muster, pretty sure she looked like an escaped clown scouting for her missing circus.

"Hello," she called. "What can I get you two?"

Ugh, Mr. Gourmet had already eaten a croissant

and a scone. Smooth. Probably he didn't want anything else.

But the lady smiled at her with a glint in her dark eyes Claire couldn't interpret.

"You must be Claire."

"Yes, I am."

Something wasn't adding up here. Had she met this woman before? Was *she* the Wandering Gourmet, and she'd sent her friend/husband/boyfriend into the bakery ahead of her as a scout?

The lady laid a hand on her own chest and patted it. "I'm Dr. Carlton's receptionist. He suggested that me and my husband come in."

"Oh," Claire said as everything fell apart and came back together in two point two seconds. So much for the Wandering Gourmet theory. Of course Eric had sent them in.

Then Marco joined the party, calling over Claire's shoulder, "So you're not a restaurant critic?" in the world's worst Captain Obvious moment.

Mr. Gourmet, who was not in any way, shape, or form associated with gourmet after all, said, "Excuse me? I'm an accountant."

That explained the way he evaluated everything. Probably calculating the asset value. A habit or something.

"Great," Marco whispered heatedly. "That's all we need."

"Excuse me," Claire said with a smile that was more gritted teeth than anything and pushed on

Marco's chest to get him to back up. All the way behind the counter.

But not fast enough to avoid hearing Mr. Accountant tell his wife, "You know, the food is good. But the service is a little peculiar."

To cap it all off, Claire's mom breezed into the bakery with her serious-talk face on. Great, that was exactly what she needed right now. Another Italy crisis. That was all her mother could talk about lately, how Dad wanted to put her out to pasture before she was ready. The trip would mark the beginning of the end of her life, yadda yadda.

Seriously, Claire couldn't handle all of this at once, not right now.

"Mom, could you just…please—"

And then Helen took one look at the couple Claire was talking to and wheeled on one heel to promptly exit the bakery. Fabulous. Now her mother's feelings were hurt.

"Just one second," Claire said with a saccharine smile that felt as forced as it was.

Helen gestured broadly as Claire joined her on the street. "I completely forgot I have a showing."

That was weird. She hadn't even been expecting her mother. But now that she was here, an intense need to talk about the thing on *her* mind wouldn't leave her alone. "Okay, well. Call me later? I have good news."

"What?"

The showing must not be that important. And she really didn't want to wait anyway. Claire grabbed her mother's hands, totally unable to hide her glee. "I talked to Eric, and we're all getting together this weekend."

Her mother's smile shattered. "We are?"

"I thought you'd be excited."

What was this day all about? Critics who were accountants, and Eric's receptionist causing her mother to misinterpret the entire situation.

"I am," her mother insisted a beat too late. "Very excited. Gotta go."

Helen took off down the brick pavers toward Boston Street and then quickly veered back the way she'd come to cross against the light, as if she'd truly forgotten where she'd parked.

Claire couldn't worry about her mother's bizarre behavior. She had customers. None of whom seemed to be the Wandering Gourmet, but they were all paying her bills, so there was that.

Helen easily found the spot at the park near the hospital that Eric had mentioned in his text message. What wasn't easy? Getting out of the car and going to a secret rendezvous with her daughter's boyfriend, whom she wasn't even supposed to have met yet.

What a mess.

Eric's face when he caught sight of her reflected the exact same sentiment. He unfolded from his casual lounge to stand there, arms crossed, glowering at her.

"I'm sorry!" she called out in advance of reaching him. The situation warranted an offensive approach.

Eric gave her a grim smile, clearly not interested in chit-chat either. "Why didn't you just tell her?"

He'd started walking along the path toward the bridge that spanned the small waterway running through the center of the park. A lovely spot. Unless you were being called on the carpet for both creating the mess and then not cleaning it up like you'd promised you would.

There wasn't anything for Helen to do but walk with Eric as she struggled to find the words to explain.

"I tried to tell her." In her defense, she'd opened her mouth at least four times to blurt out the truth. "But she kept talking about you and how happy she was. I just didn't have the heart. Or the courage. Take your pick."

She didn't have any trouble being honest with Eric. Why was it so different with Claire? Because she knew what her daughter's reaction was going to be, and it wasn't a pretty picture.

Claire had told her to butt out. And she hadn't. It was more than a mess. It was a breach of trust.

"The longer we wait—"

"I know," she broke in before Eric could finish the sentiment. "I know."

Saying it didn't make it magically fixed, though.

"I went to the bakery today," she threw in. "To try to tell her again, but Donna from your office was there."

"What?" Eric's voice had gone up a whole octave. "Did she say anything?"

"I have no idea. The second I saw her, I hightailed out of there."

"This is not going to end well," Eric predicted bleakly.

Yeah, already knew that one. Helen paused at the center of the bridge, staring out over the water, but she barely saw the pretty multi-level landscaping that edged the small canal.

"It looks like my meddling has finally ruined everything," she said in a tiny voice.

Eric joined her at the railing. "No. Look if it wasn't for you, I never would have met Claire in the first place. So for that, thank you."

He was far too generous. More than a woman about to be put out to the pasture of retirement deserved, anyway. Sam was still upset with her about Italy, and as soon as Claire found out the truth about Eric, she'd lose her daughter too.

Having a thriving real estate business suddenly felt like a very poor substitute for being a wife and mother.

Sixteen

THE ITALIAN MARBLE BIRDBATH DIDN'T resemble the Greco-Roman style Sam had been promised by a slick marketing campaign designed to relieve him of several hundred dollars. It was actually kind of ugly with two carved kids, a boy and a girl, in a sort-of hug. The statue dominated the tiny front yard that kept him from having to spend all day Saturday cutting the grass.

So much for this project. At least it hadn't started raining while he'd set it up.

As he took a step back to hopefully find an angle that made it look less horrendous, Arnie drove up. Unexpectedly. But it was a nice surprise.

"Hey," Sam called as Arnie emerged from his Mercedes.

"Hey." Arnie stepped gingerly into the grass to stand by Sam, both of them staring at the monstrosity. "Looks good."

"Nice try, Arnie. It's ridiculous." If he couldn't laugh at his own taste, who could? "I ordered it a

month ago as a surprise for Helen. It didn't seem so…
big online."

He'd never imagined that such a thing would make
it look like he was trying too hard. When he'd gone in
search of something she might like, he'd had zero clue
they'd be tiptoeing around each other so much at this
point. That they'd barely be speaking outside of polite
greetings and simple communicative statements like
I'm going for a run.

"Ah, it's nice," Arnie said easily, ever the peace-
maker, just like when they were kids. "She'll love it."

The pause lengthened, and Sam glanced at his
brother, who was surely here for a reason.

"Listen, Sam, I need to talk to you about something," he finally said.

That sounded bad. Maybe Sam shouldn't be so
quick to assume that everything was going great in his
brother's world.

"What's up?" Sam shoved his hands in the pockets
of his jacket.

"Well, I was running some errands downtown,
and, uh… I hope I'm doing the right thing." Arnie
shook his head, his expression grave. "I saw Helen
walking in the park."

This was about *Helen*? "Yeah? So?"

"She was with a man," Arnie stressed as if this
might change everything for Sam.

It didn't. "Sure. She meets with clients all the
time."

And it was always perfectly innocent. Sam would
stake his life on that.

"This looked like more than just a client," his brother insisted.

"Oh, Arnie. Whatever it is, it isn't what you're thinking."

Sam almost laughed at how misguided this whole conversation was. If there was anything he knew about Helen, it was that she took her vows seriously. They might be having trouble getting on the right page about the next twenty years of their life, but it wasn't because Helen had alternate plans with another man.

"I took a picture of them with my phone." Arnie pulled out a piece of paper and handed it to him. "I printed out a copy."

Sam unfolded it. The quality of the photo wasn't great, but Sam could identify Helen blindfolded if the situation called for it, and it was definitely her. With a man, as advertised, but he had to be twenty years younger than his wife—or more. And they were just talking. Maybe standing a little closer together than might be socially acceptable for a client, but there were a thousand reasons that could be.

Like, maybe the guy was hard of hearing. Or he was actually the son of a friend, whom Helen had met before. Or her earring had fallen off, and he'd leaned in to hand it back to her.

Probably it was none of those. But it wasn't what Arnie thought. There was no way.

"I'm sorry, Sam," Arnie said after a beat.

"Look." He pointed at the photo as a funny feeling crawling up his spine. "I have no idea who he is. But trust me. It's not what you think."

It never was with Helen. Even he couldn't always read her mind, and he'd had thirty years of practice.

"Sure about that?" his brother asked incredulously.

"Very sure." Sam snorted. "But if I know my wife, she's definitely up to something."

"Like what?"

"That's what I intend to find out."

This guy meant *something* to Helen. He could feel it. She'd been so distracted lately, and if this man had something to do with it, Sam wanted to know what it was. If nothing else, maybe solving this mystery would get him closer to figuring out how to reconnect with his wife.

Italy certainly wasn't cutting it. Neither was an ill-advised birdbath. But something had to be the answer.

He glanced at his watch as Arnie waved goodbye, having done his duty. Helen had texted him that she planned to stop at the grocery store on the way home, so he took her absence as an opportunity to snoop.

The study, which he rarely used much anymore now that he'd passed all his clients off to Richard, sat silently in almost perfect order. He rifled through some stuff in the basket on top of the desk. Boring title paperwork and a few glossy brochures of houses in Helen's portfolio. In other words, nothing helpful.

Her computer password had been Claire1005, a combination of their daughter's name and birthday, for a million years, and none of the warnings he'd given her about online security seemed to sink in.

Today, he blessed her stubbornness, since it allowed him to easily log in to see what she'd been up to.

Boy, Helen didn't make it hard at all to figure out what had occupied her thoughts over the last few weeks.

She'd left her browser open to the dating site she'd been pursuing. Page after page of young, mostly dark-haired men scrolled across the screen. Sam touched his own silver hair. It was enough to give a guy a complex—if any of this had been evidence that his wife was actually cheating on him.

There had to be another explanation, and when he clicked on the user profile, he discovered it. In spades. That was *Claire's* picture and bio, not Helen's. His jaw dropped—and not figuratively, either. The real deal, with a mouth open wide enough to catch flies.

"Unbelievable."

She'd been posing as Claire to meet men through an online dating service.

That made a whole lot more sense than the idea that Helen was meeting these much-younger men as herself. Relieved that he had an answer to his wife's bizarre behavior, he started to shut down the computer.

Wait just a minute. What happened when she met one? Clearly that was what Arnie had seen at the park downtown. How in the world did his wife explain herself when these men realized she wasn't Claire?

Footsteps echoed from the stairs.

"Sam, I'm home," Helen called.

Great timing. His lovely wife had a lot of explaining to do. *A lot.*

He grabbed the picture of the man Helen had met on Claire's behalf and stalked to the first floor. Helen stood at the island in the center of the whitewashed kitchen, pulling groceries out of the cloth bag she'd carried to the market.

"I picked up some salmon," she said as he entered. "I thought we could marinate it in a mustard sauce."

She crossed to stick the paper-wrapped package in the fridge, catching sight of his face, which made her do a double take.

"I'm guessing you're not in the mood for fish?" she said with a lift at the end that turned it into a question.

"We need to talk," he told her firmly.

If this matchmaking business was the reason Helen had been off the idea of Italy, they had much more to talk about than just the fact that it was creepy to pose as your own daughter to meet men on her behalf. Besides, Claire had a boyfriend. What was Helen doing? Trying to find a backup in case that didn't work out?

"Is this about Italy?" she asked with a sigh that didn't improve his mood.

"Italy is the least of our problems."

Calmly, she set a bunch of celery on the counter. "What are you talking about?"

"I'm talking about George. And Neal."

"Who?" Her voice had gone squeaky, an admission of guilt if he'd ever heard one.

"And this guy in the park." He shoved the picture

toward her and waited until she took it. "How could you do this to your own daughter?"

"How did you get this?"

That was Helen's shocked face. Good. He'd knocked her off balance. Now maybe they'd get somewhere. "Arnie saw you two together. Who is this guy?"

"That's Eric."

"Claire's boyfriend?"

Wow. This went way beyond creepy to a place he didn't even know how to describe. He tossed the picture on the counter.

"Sam, I was only trying to help," she called as he stalked back out of the kitchen, too beleaguered to come up with anything more to say that might fix this bizarre situation.

After a tense dinner, he asked Helen to go for a walk since the skies seemed to be holding back the rain for now. They were married, and she deserved a chance to explain herself. The fact that he'd never in a million years have guessed that *for better or worse* would cover a mom creating an online dating profile on behalf of her daughter notwithstanding.

Silence stretched as they rounded the corner at the end of their street full of Craftsman-style houses they both loved.

It seemed like a million years ago they'd bought their dream house on this block. Helen had told him about this listing the moment it had popped up on her radar, and it had felt like the right place for them instantly. The closing had been effortless. Just like the bulk of their relationship.

That was why this distance between them had taken its toll. At least on his side. They'd always been so close, not one of those couples who fought constantly. They rarely even got cross with each other.

And he wasn't going to give up until he'd fixed it. Understanding the scheme that had apparently taken up a lot of Helen's headspace over the last little while was step one.

"Start talking," he told her with no room for argument this time.

She sighed. "I went online posing as Claire in hopes of finding her a date. As soon as they found out it was her mother, they ran for the hills."

"As they should have." Because it was nuts. But at least she was talking, so he shut up.

"Eric was sitting at the bar, watching all of this. We struck up a conversation, and ten minutes in, I knew he was the one for Claire."

Sam shook his head. "This is so wrong in *so* many ways."

"Oh, I know." Helen's frame fairly vibrated with tension as they walked, another thing he'd like to fix, but it was on her to keep up the momentum at this point. "They're so perfect together, and I may have ruined it."

Well, that was unfortunate, but that was what happened when you did wacky stuff. "You have to tell Claire. I'm serious, Helen. If you don't, I will. And this new obsession with matchmaking has to stop."

Helen paused near the Wenneker's mailbox.

"Actually, I've been matchmaking since the day we met."

"What are you talking about?" A ploy to get off this subject, or even get her off the hook?

"That day at the bookstore. There was another copy of *A Room with a View*. You were so nice and I wanted to get to know you, so I hid the other copy."

Sam blinked, but the earnest expression on his wife's face didn't change. "So my favorite story about us is a lie. Great."

And the hits kept on coming. Maybe they'd been on different paths a lot longer than he'd assumed.

"I've been carrying around that secret for thirty-four years," she said softly.

"You'll forgive me if I don't sympathize with your burden."

"Well, maybe this is a better story," she countered, her voice a bit stronger as she warmed to this new reality. "I had an instant crush and I acted fast. And here we are, a lifetime later. Still in love. Say what you will about my methods, but sometimes I do get it right."

And maybe she wasn't far off. There was a time not so long ago—as in, the last five minutes—when he wouldn't have laid odds on her still being in love with him. It was nice to hear that confirmation.

Maybe knowing the truth about how they'd met did add something instead of taking away from their relationship. After all, her methods included knowing what she wanted and going for it. The thing he liked about her best. Since he'd been the object of her affection, how could he complain?

"I doubt your daughter sees it that way." He stopped walking and faced her, determined to put his money where his mouth was. "You know, that day we met. You didn't have to manipulate fate. I never would've let you go."

Something warm and heavy cloaked them both, gathering them up in its wake, pulling them together where nothing else had.

They had a lovely moment where they were in perfect cohesion, the way they'd been for decades. The way that had been missing for a while. He savored it. While it lasted, anyway.

Helen nodded toward the monstrosity of marble in their front yard. "If we could make a wish at that fountain, what would you wish for?"

"An honest wife."

She laughed softly, with self-effacing humor. "You said that too fast."

"How about you? Would you want a wish?"

Her answer came instantly, along with a misty smile. "Another thirty-four years with the love of my life."

They'd turned a corner. Sam could feel it in the way she was looking at him, the pressure of her hand on his arm. Somehow, her confessions had lightened things between them. Maybe this all had been weighing her down to the point that it had started to interfere with their relationship. If so, he was glad he'd forced the issues out into the open.

Nothing was settled or fixed, but for the first time, he had hope they could get there. As soon as Claire knew the truth, maybe he'd have his wife's attention back.

They strolled arm in arm up the driveway, right by the monstrosity. He couldn't help but remark, "It really is big, isn't it?"

"Mmm," Helene murmured noncommittally. Which was why their marriage had lasted.

She knew when to talk and when no words could possibly cover it.

Seventeen

AFTER A LONG DAY FULL of appointments and one side trip to the hospital to provide a second opinion on an experimental pediatric procedure, all Eric wanted to do was sit on the couch and eat the spaghetti he'd made.

Of course, his phone rang a half second after he'd dumped the noodles on his plate. He glanced at it, pretty sure he wasn't going to answer. Except it was Claire's mom.

A very bad feeling swam through the pit of his stomach, which didn't pair well with spaghetti. He answered.

"Eric, it's me," Helen muttered under her breath. "Sam knows."

"What?" Of all the things she could've said, that was not what he'd expected.

"He says he's going to tell Claire."

Well, if Helen had already told her—like she should have—this wouldn't even be an issue. "I knew this would happen."

Like he'd been predicting to her time and time

again. This simply escalated the point. They had to do damage control. Stat.

And he was done letting Helen drive that bus. Claire deserved to learn the truth, and she was going to hear it from Eric. It might already be too late to salvage their relationship, but man, he hoped that wasn't true.

He really wanted to have this whole fiasco behind them. So they could move forward. Everything with Claire felt...right. As if he'd finally found the one woman who worked in his life.

Only to have the threat of losing her hanging over his head. No more.

Eric drove to Gilded Sweets without bothering to swing by Claire's house. She wouldn't be there. Frankly, she should take his half-serious advice to stick a futon in the back room of the bakery; there was almost no point in paying for her condo when she was never there.

The lights were off in the front when he got there, and a quick tug on the glass door proved that it was locked. Good. He hated the idea of Claire being here alone this late.

He hated the idea of interrupting her solitude even more. She liked being by herself in her bakery, as she'd told him on several occasions. It helped goose her creativity. And as her official taste tester, he benefited from her new creations, so he bit his tongue when it came to her hours.

He truly didn't mind finding creative ways to spend time with her as she built up her own business. Whenever they were together, they seemed so in tune with one another, in a way he hadn't felt with any woman he'd dated before. The bakery gave him a place to come to in order to hang out and still see her, and she never minded if he had patients to see first.

They were a match made in workaholic heaven.

It doubled his resolve to get the truth out into the open and see where the chips fell. If Claire felt half as strongly about him as he did about her, she might find a way to be forgiving of him too. It could happen.

The review of their finances hadn't gone well. Claire dropped the tray full of leftover pastries from the front case onto the silver prep table in the kitchen. It clattered something fierce, fitting her mood.

Marco, who had already changed out of his white chef coat into his street clothes, joined her in the kitchen, his expression a touch less grim than it had been a few minutes ago—when they'd arrived at the simultaneous conclusion that they were barely making ends meet.

Never mind taking it to the next level, like they'd dreamed for so long.

"I know I'm preaching to the choir, but this review could make or break us," Marco said, in a continuation of the conversation they hadn't had earlier but should have.

She couldn't bear to talk like that, though. Sure, the books weren't looking pretty, but the profits were better than they ever had been, thanks to the side jobs her mom had gotten them.

"Okay, well maybe we can take a few more catering gigs to keep us afloat until the Wandering Gourmet wanders our way."

That meant more cancelled dates with Eric. But only for a little while. There was a light at the end of this tunnel, and it wasn't a train.

"What if we're counting on something that's never going to happen?" Marco spread his arms wide in obvious frustration.

Which she felt too, but airing such pessimism didn't help anyone. "I need you to stay positive, partner."

"Aye-aye, captain." He gave her a half-hearted salute. "I think I'll wander home. See you in the morning."

"All right."

Now that Marco was gone, she couldn't keep her smile fixed in place. Her eyelids fluttered closed as she contemplated all the ways this had been a super-long day. A long slog uphill as a whole, and not just today. First with trying to get Gilded Sweets off the ground and then to keep it in business while at the mercy of Seattle diners' whims.

"I can't give up on you," she said to the bakery walls. "I won't."

A silly thing, to talk to your building. But she'd swear it could hear her. That was yet another reason she tried to stay positive. If the bakery sensed she might be crumbling, it would be like giving it permission to follow suit.

Not happening. Not on her watch.

As she walked back toward the front to be sure she'd gathered all the leftover pastries, someone knocked on the back door, the one delivery people usually used. But it was too late for that, and Marco had a key.

"Hello?" she called, waiting for the knocker to identify themselves before opening the door.

"It's me. It's Eric."

That was the one voice she'd wished to hear. Immediately, she unlocked the deadbolt to admit him. The first sight of his gorgeous face filled her on the inside in a way that pastries never had. Not an unwelcome thing, but a little scary. How had she not realized how important he'd become to her?

"Hey. I hope you start making a habit out of this."

She meant it, too. There was something so nice about the combination of Eric and the bakery, as if the building approved of him as well.

"I'd like to," he said with the tiniest break in his voice as if her comment had struck him in a gooey place inside.

Well, good. He made her gooey too, and she wasn't about to ask him to stop.

"Do you want some napoleons or cherry scones? Take your pick."

She'd much rather give them to Eric than throw them out. She died a little each time she had to toss her creations in the garbage, because they weren't trash. Just forlorn and unwanted, which was exactly the opposite of why she'd baked the treat in the first place.

"Maybe later," he said in his deep, rich voice that sent a good shiver down her spine.

"Okay, well how about the hospital? We could bring them to the kids." Still one of her favorite memories and definitely the best first date on record.

"Not tonight."

"All right. I just have to get something from the front." And then maybe they could have a good long conversation over tea, like the way they'd done the first time Eric had come to the bakery late at night.

He followed her. "Claire, there's something I need to tell you."

The lights flickered above them with an ominous buzz, cutting him off.

Great. Eric had finally gotten up the nerve to lay everything out, and the electricity had chosen to punctuate his statement with a threatening crackle. He couldn't let it distract him.

"Ugh. This happens all the time," Claire said, staring at the ceiling. "Just another thing to fix. And pay for."

They emerged into the dim seating area on the customer side of the counter. Safety lights glowed from the ceiling and along the floor, so the power seemed to be back to normal.

He swallowed against the big ball of nerves in his throat and tried again. He had to get this out and also not screw up everything. Tall order. "Yeah. So, look, I wanted to tell you...about the night we met."

She paused swinging around to face him, her face lit from above by the soft lights. "It was very romantic."

"Yes, it was very romantic," he agreed, struck all at once how much that actually meant to him. He wouldn't have called himself a romantic, not by a long shot.

But that didn't change facts. He'd found Claire against some pretty strong odds, and it was important for her to understand that while their meeting might be unorthodox, that didn't negate the fact that they *had* met.

That meant something, too. To both of them. He felt sure of it.

"But," he said, determined to plow on. "It wasn't by accident."

"So you agree with me, then," she said with a charming smile as the lights buzzed and flickered again.

Distracted, he glanced at the ceiling and then back at Claire. "Sorry, agree with what?"

"That it was fate that brought us together."

No. Not even close. He had to get her off the fate train and back into the realm of reality—namely, that the genesis of their relationship was the very opposite of destiny. They'd met by *design,* and that was so much better.

He opened his mouth to convince her of that

when the power gave up the ghost, plunging them both into near darkness.

Figured. He'd finally made the decision to move forward on telling Claire the truth without waiting on Helen to get around to it, and now this.

Since he couldn't see his hand in front of his face, he fished his phone from his pocket, punching up the flashlight. Which illuminated Claire holding a thick white pillar.

"Why don't we light a candle?" she suggested wryly.

"That's better."

"It is better," she said and went in search of matches, which she found near the register. Striking one, she lit the candle and handed it to him. "There you go."

She lit another one and grinned up at him as if a power outage was the most fun she'd had all week. And normally, he might agree. Speaking of romantic... The lit candles and the hush of the restaurant made for a compelling atmosphere to do anything but address the elephant in the room.

Which was exactly what he wanted to do—ignore the elephant. Just for a moment longer so he could bask in Claire. She was so beautiful and funny and brilliant. Easily the best thing that had happened to him in a long time.

"What do we do?" she murmured, clearly struck by the same sense of awareness he'd noted.

"I don't know, I'm just a doctor," he admitted.

"Well, I'm just a baker," she countered with a

laugh. "So clearly two professions that are completely useless in this situation."

And all at once, she leaned in and kissed him, for no apparent reason other than because she wanted to. Which he heartily approved of. He might have even gone back for seconds after she pulled away.

Bad, bad idea.

Except it jogged his brain into recalling a bit about how electricity worked. "That's it. The breaker box. Where's the breaker box?"

"Oh, you are smart." She tapped his chest. "This way."

Her steps slowed as she entered the back room, her laughter dying instantly as she took in the darkened room. "The lights are off in the kitchen. I need to check the fridge."

Faster now, she darted to the giant silver industrial cooler. Eric could hardly keep up as he followed her, his heart trying to climb out of his chest as he worked on balancing the situation at hand against his desire to have everything right between them.

"Ugh, it's off," she called from inside the cavernous cooler. "Everything is going to spoil. I have to call my mom. She knows a good electrician."

No! She couldn't call Helen. What if her father answered and spilled everything? He quickened his steps and crashed straight into a...something that clattered to the floor. And almost took him with it.

But he recovered. Not gracefully. Enough to stay off the ground. So there was that.

Candle. He'd dropped it. A *lit candle* was rolling

around on Claire's kitchen. That would be a fantastic end to this fiasco—a visit from the Lake Union fire department.

"Are you okay?" she called as he stooped to pick up the wax pillar, which wasn't actually lit anymore, thankfully.

"Yeah. Yeah, I'm good," he croaked as he climbed to his feet.

Too late. Claire had her phone glued to her ear already.

Helen pressed the phone closer as she strained to hear the conversation on Claire's end.

"Who did you call?" a male voice asked.

"My mom," Claire said but not to her.

"Who was that?" Helen demanded, her voice echoing in the dining room as she crossed through it.

"Eric."

A shiver slid down her spine. She pivoted, unable to stop pacing. "He's *there*?"

That…that *traitor*. He'd gone straight over to Gilded Sweets after talking to her. Likely to ruin everything, all because Helen had lacked the conviction to tell Claire the truth herself.

She sighed, deflating a little. Maybe that was for the best.

"Yes," Claire stressed. "The lights went out in the bakery."

"I'll call my electrician and send him over." Helen paused for a beat. "Are you okay?"

What she meant was, *did Eric say anything,* but it wasn't like she could come right out and ask, just in case he hadn't.

"No," Claire snapped, giving Helen a mild coronary. "The electricity went out."

"But…" Helen drew it out as she struggled to ask the million-dollar question without really asking it. "Nothing *else* is wrong?"

"Isn't that enough?"

Claire ended the call as Helen took a breath to say something else—anything else. Beeps emanated from the phone. She stared at it for a second as a few more tendrils of panic unfurled in her chest.

"Sam," she called, and he glanced up from his book, his cute reading glasses turning his eyes a pretty color. "She's with *Eric.*"

And how nice it was that she could talk to Sam about this mess. After weeks of keeping this secret, it was a relief to not have to watch what she said or dodge phone calls from her daughter's boyfriend. Who was even now possibly tearing a hole in her relationship with Claire.

"Did he tell her about your matchmaking?" her husband asked calmly.

Trust Sam to cut right to the chase. "Apparently not. Maybe I can have the electrician tell her."

Wouldn't it be nice if that solved everything? She scrolled through her contacts to find the retired firefighter who'd reinvented himself as an electrician.

She'd recommended him to all her clients who needed repair work done prior to listing their houses and had never gotten a thing other than glowing reviews about his services.

"Joke all you want, but you have to deal with this. You, not Eric." He flipped a hand in her direction and went back to his book. "This is your mess."

"I know." And she was ruining his reading time with her obsessiveness. "I just don't know how, or when, or what to say."

"More importantly," Sam said, raising his head out of his book again, "how are you going to explain to her why you did it?"

Okay, *that* was the million-dollar question. Which she didn't have an answer for.

"I don't want to go there right now."

She wheeled to escape into the kitchen and realized she didn't have anything there to actually do. Blindly, she scanned the cookbook open to the chocolate chip cookie recipe she'd been planning to try, but the words blurred with suspicious moisture as she faced the only obvious answer to Sam's question.

"I guess I'd rather meddle in Claire's life than deal with my own."

Had she said that out loud? Sam's eyes were on her, so yeah. She must have. But she didn't take it back. It was the truth. Getting older was doing a number on her, and she wasn't handling it well. Look at all the angst she'd caused Sam over this Italy trip.

And now she had a giant birdbath statue on her front lawn, thanks to her waffling.

"Why don't you try telling her that?" he said. "It's a good opener."

It was. This man she'd married was a keeper for sure.

Sam deserved better. And so did Claire. It was time for Helen to grow up already and dance to the music that life had already starting playing for her instead of trying to direct the orchestra.

Eighteen

THE NEXT MORNING, CLAIRE JETTED over to her parents' house on the way to the bakery to thank her mother for calling the electrician. Marco had the bakery covered for now, especially since they weren't exactly packing the customers in.

If only the Wandering Gourmet would get off his duff and try Gilded Sweets. They'd done everything right, at least as far as they knew.

Why hadn't he come by already?

She pasted a smile on her face and lifted the box of scones from her passenger seat, carrying it with two hands up the walk. They'd survived the great power meltdown and deserved to be enjoyed.

Wow, that was a large birdbath statue gracing the front lawn. Where had that come from? It was too big for the tiny space. Almost at an in-your-face level, like someone had been trying to send a message. Her dad? About Italy?

Her mom answered the door, shock written all over her expression. "What are you doing here?"

"Can't I come by unannounced?" Claire laughed

and breezed by her mother to the kitchen, pulling a plate out of the cabinet to arrange the scones. Helen took a seat in one of the stools lining the island bar to watch.

"Your guy was great," she continued. "It took four hours, but he finally got the lights on. He said it was faulty wiring in the walls. Eric helped him out."

Helen leaned forward, her expression intent. "Speaking of Eric—"

"And then," Claire continued, because she had to get this out before she burst. "After that, he goes back to the hospital. Because a little kid has an ear infection."

"Darling—"

"I love that he's a pediatrician." If her mother would stop interrupting her, she could tell her the huge, wonderful thing that was going on inside. "I love everything about him."

She was *in love* with Eric. Last night had put the icing on that cake, without a doubt. He was strong and handsome and good-hearted. Capable. Calm in a crisis. Funny.

He'd be a great dad.

Her stomach did a little flip as she let herself imagine that for a second. She'd never had that thought about any other man she'd dated before. Eric was the one. The One in capital letters, because such a thing deserved to be emphasized.

Her own dad came into the kitchen with a tender smile for her.

"Hey, dad."

"Hey, hon," he said as he skirted her. "Your mother has something she needs to tell you."

"Well, first, you must have a scone," she told him over her shoulder as he filled his coffee cup. "I salvaged them from the fridge, so they are your reward for finding him. Thank you."

She stuck the last scone on a plate and bowed to her mom with folded hands.

"Finding who?" her mother asked with a surprised lift on the end, as if she'd already forgotten already the wonderful favor she'd done for Claire.

"The electrician. Who do you think I'm talking about?"

Claire snagged the empty scone box and turned to put it in the trash, half listening as her dad sat down at the bar next to her mom, murmuring something in her ear. They were always like that, lost in each other. For a long time, she'd been convinced she'd never find anyone who made her feel like that: as if the rest of the world didn't exist.

And then the universe had gifted her with Eric…

As she set the scone box into the trash receptacle, the piece of paper on top caught her attention. Maybe because it was so unusual to see a printed photo. Maybe because the guy in the picture looked like Eric, whom she clearly had on the brain. Maybe because it was a picture of her mother with another man, which also seemed so out of place.

But as she pulled the paper from the trash, a feeling of unease slid down her spine.

This *was* a photograph of Eric. And her mother. Together. Talking.

"Mom," she said, staring at the photo, trying to corral her thoughts. Obviously, there was a logical explanation. Because all of the ones she'd made up in her head so far didn't work. "What is this?"

Her mom glanced at her dad, the expression on her face veering between pure guilt and pure concern.

"We should talk," she said firmly. "In the living room maybe, so we'll be more comfortable."

"Maybe talk now," Claire suggested with false cheer. If she had to wait another second to get an explanation for this photo, she'd explode. As it was, her pulse had skyrocketed to rollercoaster level, and not in a good, anticipatory way. More like the way it did when you realized the first hill looked a whole lot scarier than it had before you were trapped in the car with a metal bar across your lap.

Her mother stood. "This might take a while."

Gritting her teeth, Claire followed her parents to the living room and waited until they'd both perched on the couch to lift her brows. "So. How does your trash can contain a photograph of you with my boyfriend? Whom you haven't met yet. Right?"

"Clearly I have met him," her mother said with a nervous laugh. "But I should start at the beginning."

"Please do."

Claire couldn't seem to make herself sit down. Her legs had far too much restless energy. Which did not get better as she listened to her mother explain how she'd set up an online dating profile that she'd used to meet men. Except not for herself. For *Claire*.

Because the profile was in Claire's name. With her picture. And her interests.

And somehow Eric was smack in the middle of all of this.

This was all so very *not okay*.

"So you find these guys online," Claire repeated incredulously. Because how else was she supposed to feel but confused—and more than a little shocked? "Meet them in a bar, and that's how you found Eric."

The words tasted sour in her mouth, like cream that had turned. She wanted to spit all of it out and have none of this be true. None of this made a lick of sense.

"But he wasn't one of those," her mother corrected, shaking her finger as if that made any sort of difference. "Actually, he was there on a date."

Claire blinked. He was *what*? "Okay, so he witnessed your insanity and still thought it was a good idea to meet your daughter."

No question—insanity was definitely the name of this game. Because no sane person would've gotten into the middle of any of this. Yet Eric had. Somehow.

Who was he really if not the guy she'd met at the gallery completely by chance?

Her stomach rolled as she realized she had no idea.

"Not quite," her mother explained helpfully. "I had to convince him. So I went to his office."

"You did what?" her father broke in.

"I'm trying to confess here," her mom murmured

to him. "And so I sort-of arranged for you to meet at the gallery. But I did not arrange that magical moment when you two first saw each other."

"You were there?" Claire squawked, shocked her voice had worked at all.

Her mother shifted her gaze away. "Yes."

That took the cake, the pie, and all of the tarts.

Nothing about how she'd met Eric was real. There was no romance, no magic. It was all an elaborate setup, orchestrated by her *mother*. Of all the pieces of this that she couldn't believe, that one might be the worst.

Because she'd told her mother to butt out of her love life. Several times, in fact.

A sharp pang of betrayal burned through her gut. Problem was, she couldn't decide who had the bigger role in this betrayal. Everyone in this situation had misrepresented something. Repeatedly.

"She didn't tell me that, either," her dad said. "You didn't tell me that."

Like that mattered? Apparently, her father had known about this, too, and hadn't bothered to say anything.

No one in her life could be trusted. What else didn't she know?

"Don't blame Eric, blame me." Her mother jabbed at her own chest.

Yeah, there was enough for everyone to get some. And she blamed them both. A lot. What she could not do was reconcile this new Eric she'd learned existed mere moments ago with the man she'd spent so many hours with, just the two of them…the man who loved his patients and cared so much for them. That Eric and the Eric in the photograph were not the same man.

She let her head drop into her hands. "I just can't believe he'd sign on for something so crazy."

"He wanted to tell you," her mom announced.

"Well, he had ample opportunity."

That was the hardest part of all of this. Eric had been keeping this from her the whole time. There she'd been, going on and on about how magical their meeting at the gallery had been, and he'd known the whole time that it hadn't been by chance. That he and her mother had arranged the whole thing.

There was no destiny involved. Cold calculation only. It was a kick to the gut and then some.

"He was afraid you'd be mad," her mother said in the most classic case of reading Claire's thoughts imaginable.

"I am. I am mad," she cried.

"I'm so sorry."

"So am I."

And she'd had enough of this. Claire strode from the room, too heartsick to even cry.

There was no fateful encounter at an art gallery. No story to tell her kids one day. Not only that, there wouldn't be any kids, at least not with Eric, because what he'd done was unforgivable.

Trust was a huge part of a relationship, and he'd not only broken it, but stomped all over it.

What a fool she was. Eric already knew her

mother. When she'd talked about her mom and how excited she was for him to meet her, he'd been laughing to himself. The whole time.

How stupid was she to have believed she'd finally gotten all of her romance boxes checked?

Blindly, she drove to the bakery. Muffins didn't bake themselves and besides, where else was she supposed to go? The bakery was the only thing she had left that wasn't a lie.

By the end of the day, Claire counted her lucky stars that the bakery was still standing and hadn't succumbed to one of many disasters she'd seemed bent on creating. She'd burned *two* pans of croissants—*two whole pans*! And not at the same time, either. On the first batch, she'd forgotten to set a timer. Then on the second batch, she'd set the oven to the wrong temperature.

This is your chef with relationship woes, everyone. Look out.

Not to be outdone, she'd then gone on to mischarge three customers in a row, all of whom had pointed it out after she'd handed them their credit card receipt. She might as well have *Idiot* emblazoned across her chef's smock.

That was what she felt like. Constantly. It wouldn't ease no matter what she did.

Defeated and feeling pretty forlorn, she wandered out to dump a bag of trash in the dumpster and then just…couldn't with life anymore. Her legs wouldn't hold her up a second longer.

She sank onto the bench hugging the exterior back wall of the bakery. If she never budged from this spot, she never had to face her new reality.

Except sitting in the alleyway didn't halt the barrage of everything. Eric wasn't the man she'd thought he was. How could she have been so stupid as to think that fate would work in her favor when it hadn't any other time?

Worse, her mother never gave fate any breathing room. She had to be right in the middle of everything, pulling strings, ensuring that Claire danced to her tune.

She'd been doing the same thing to Claire's father. That was why they weren't going to Italy, after all. Her mother had let him believe in that, too, then had pulled the rug out from under him by announcing she wasn't ready to retire—after he'd given all his clients to Richard.

Claire's heart ached for her dad, for his dreams that her mother had broken.

But that was how Helen operated, apparently. And Claire had been too blind to see it.

Or rather, she'd known that her mother liked to have her hand in everything that went on. Dresses, napkins, what Claire had ultimately ended up doing as her profession. Even baking had its roots in how she'd been brought up. In the kitchen, by her mother's side.

Marco found her in the alleyway. He was already

dressed in his street clothes, which meant she must've been out here longer than she'd thought.

He settled onto the bench gingerly, probably worried he'd send her off on a crying jag or something. That would be par for the course today.

"We could always put up a sign," he offered. "'Closed due to heartbreak.'"

That sounded like a fabulous idea. But a totally unfair one. It wasn't Marco's fault her life had fallen apart.

"I'll be fine," she told him and almost meant it. "Maybe."

"That bad, huh?"

"I don't know." Marco was so patient. A kind soul, and his concern nearly broke her. "I think I convinced myself I had all the time in the world to find the man of my dreams. And suddenly, he's right in front of me. The fairy tale begins. But lo and behold, my mother has orchestrated the entire thing."

That was the part that had gutted her. She hadn't been looking for Eric. That was what had made it so special that she'd found him. Like her own personal gift from the universe. *You've worked hard, Claire. You deserve something good for yourself. Have this amazing man who's beautiful and kind and everything you never knew you wanted.*

"Nothing is ever just my own," she told him. Anguish rose in her throat, making her voice crack. "And this time, I just don't know that I can forgive her."

Her phone rang again. *Eric.* She didn't have to glance

at the screen to know she'd see his name emblazoned across it. Obviously, her mother had clued him in that the truth had come out, because he'd called eight times already. She toyed with the idea of blocking his number but didn't have the energy.

Instead she set the phone back down on the bench face-down.

Marco glanced at the phone and then her face. "Was that Eric or your mother?"

"Eric." Not that it mattered.

"Sooner or later, you're going to have to talk to him," he said, which was a perfectly reasonable point.

He deserved a chance to explain his side. Didn't he?

She blew out a breath. "I will."

If for no other reason than to ask him the question burning inside her—what would have been wrong with telling her at the gallery that her mother had sent him? He could have said he'd come out of curiosity, but now that he'd met her, he could tell they'd have something special.

That might have been as romantic as a meeting by chance. A story she could still tell her kids.

That was what was killing her. Not only had he not done that, he hadn't said one word in all the days since. Why? Because he was afraid she'd be *mad*? So… he hadn't planned on saying anything ever?

That was even more unforgivable than what her mom had done.

"But," she clarified, "not until I figure out what I'm going to do."

Marco nodded. "Okay. I'm going. Need a lift?"

"No, I'm good." Or as good as it seemed she was going to get tonight.

The tears kind of ruined the validity of her statement though. She wiped her eyes, but thankfully Marco didn't comment on it.

"See you in the morning?"

"Yeah." She sniffed and turned her phone off. There was no point in staring at the eight missed calls.

Nineteen

From across the square, Eric watched as Claire pushed open the glass door and lugged an easel-style sign onto the sidewalk. Normally, he'd spring forward to insist on carrying the heavy sign for her, set it up, and maybe pull Claire into his arms for an early morning hug.

This was not a normal day. For starters, he hadn't slept more than about an hour last night. He was used to running on fumes, but usually due to being at the hospital all night. Not because the woman he'd fallen in love with refused to take his calls.

She looked so good. And so bad at the same time. Beautiful, but clearly she hadn't slept much more than he had. His fault. He wanted so badly to tell her... everything. All the things in his heart. How sorry he was.

His feet moved toward her almost automatically. He certainly hadn't registered any conscious decision to approach her, and really, he hadn't quite worked out what he was even going to say.

She lifted her chin and caught sight of him, freezing him in his tracks. She paused too, for a half second, her expression snapping closed. Then she utterly dismissed him, glancing away as she moved the sign farther away from the front door, placing it where the foot traffic would see it best.

Once it was set up, she shoved her hands in her pockets as he continued to approach her, mostly because he couldn't think of anything else to do at this stage. But she didn't turn and run, just stood there staring past him as if he didn't exist.

"I had to see you," he told her, thrilled his voice still worked.

"I have a long day ahead of me," she said, finally looking at him.

He kind of wished she hadn't. The look in her eye—it was so flat. Unemotional. As if she'd already wiped away all her feelings for him.

That was when he fully internalized how badly he'd messed up.

"I can come back tonight," he offered. *Tomorrow.* The next day. Any hour of any day. As long as she picked a time that he could explain.

"I don't think that's a good idea." She still wouldn't quite look at him, her gaze darting around at the traffic in the square, as if the sight of him was causing her distress. "I just need some time to figure this out."

That didn't sound good. Or like it would end up in his favor. *Their* favor. That was what he needed to explain. That he loved her and would do whatever it took to get past this horrible place they were at.

"We really need to talk—"

"I'm not even talking to my mother right now," Claire announced with painfully clear enunciation. "And she's my best friend. Or my worst enemy, I'm not really sure which one anymore."

"I just… I feel we owe it to ourselves to see where this goes. Don't you?"

Oh, brilliant. That covered everything, didn't it? *Hey, Claire, I know you're upset, but just push all of that aside and step up.*

She stared at him, so much hurt crowded into her gaze that he almost wished she'd switch back to the flat, unemotional vacancy of a moment ago. But he'd gotten exactly what he deserved for listening to Helen and taking her cues on when to tell Claire.

That was what he wanted to tell her. That he'd insisted Helen come clean on multiple occasions and she hadn't. That he was sorry he hadn't pushed the issue. Sorry he hadn't told her himself at any of the times he'd planned to, but he hadn't because Helen had begged him to hold off.

But he didn't say that, because it was more important for Claire to mend her relationship with her mother than it was for her to forgive him.

The last thing he could live with would be if he and Claire somehow worked things out and she still refused to speak to her mom. Then that would be his fault, too.

"I'm sorry," she said. "I can't do this."

"Claire—"

And then she turned and walked away, vanishing from the sidewalk and his life.

That was when it started raining. Not the light drizzle that happened almost every day, but an earnest downpour, the kind meteorologists measured in inches. And he'd left his umbrella in the car.

By the time he got to work, he was wet and miserable. So of course the first thing he saw when he pulled out his phone was a text from Helen to meet her under the pavilion outside the hospital.

Since the rain had already soaked his clothes and his first appointment of the day had cancelled, why not? This time, he grabbed his umbrella.

I can't do this.

Claire's voice echoed in his chest, sinking its barbs into all the tender places inside.

It wasn't until he stepped under the pavilion awning that he realized he hadn't actually opened the umbrella. Because he was a class-A moron. Not that he'd needed any additional proof.

"She won't talk to me," Helen offered by way of greeting.

"Won't talk to me, either," he admitted.

"Let's make a pact. Whoever she forgives first, we'll get her to forgive the other."

Seriously, Helen? "I don't think you and I should be making any more pacts."

She sighed and meandered toward the railing that surrounded the pavilion. "You're right."

"You don't have anything to worry about though. She's going to forgive you." At least he'd done his part to ensure that happened. "You're her mother."

Whom he really shouldn't be talking to. It was

kind of nice, in a weird way, to have this small connection with Claire still. But these clandestine meetings with Helen were what had landed him in this mess.

"I know how Claire feels," Helen mused. "I felt the same way about my mother. She was always telling me what to do. Always trying to plan my life. But she meant well."

And Helen did, too. Eric knew that. The anguish in the woman's voice signified it as well, and there was no point in beating herself up. "Sounds to me like you're just repeating her behavior."

"Is that your medical opinion, Doctor?"

At least she still had a sense of humor. He'd do well to keep his intact also. "I do deal with a lot of moms."

"What about your mom?" she asked out of the blue.

"She is *very* opinionated. Warm. Funny." He glanced at Helen. "Who does that remind me of?"

Helen smiled, looking so much like Claire in that moment that it was almost painful. Honestly, a part of him had hoped Claire would be a lot like Helen. And they were very alike in many respects.

That was the other thing he would have told Claire. If she'd actually listen to him. That the reason he'd gone to the gallery that night might have had a lot more to do with Helen than he'd credited. She was a strong woman who went after what she wanted— her daughter's happiness.

Helen hadn't quit until she'd found the right match. Eric wouldn't give up that match so easily, either.

"How about that guy in the corner." Marco pointed while trying to hide behind the glass dome covering the donuts Claire always kept on top of the display case. "The one with the bow tie."

She glanced over to the table near the fireplace he'd indicated, where a single man sat writing in a notebook. He wore a dark blue blazer with tan dress pants, both of which were pressed within an inch of their lives. The Lake Union crowd usually leaned more toward bohemian and funky chic, but this guy looked like he'd stepped out of a snooty British university—or a snooty restaurant.

Oh, yeah. That was the Wandering Gourmet. For sure. "Well, his arrogance certainly fits the profile."

"Okay." Marco exhaled heavily. "So we'll just be really, really nice to him."

Claire slid an empty dish from the display case and stuck it out of sight. "Oh, of course. Because we're usually so rude to our customers."

"Oh, come on. You know that's not what I mean."

The door chimed, admitted a dark-haired woman with a kind face, who glanced around as if looking for someone.

"She looks familiar," Claire murmured, her gaze narrowing as she tried to place the woman. "I think she's one of my mom's friends."

Probably sent as a spy. Claire straightened her spine. If that was her mom's game, fine. But this advanced reconnaissance mission wasn't going to win her mother any points, because Claire wasn't going to engage. At all.

"Okay, I'll take her," Marco said, because he truly was a good friend who just got it when Claire needed him to most. "You concentrate on Bow Tie. Offer him something not on the menu."

Great idea. It would make Gilded Sweets seem a lot more cosmopolitan. What did she have in the fridge that she could whip up easily? Cream and maybe some bacon? Ugh, what could she do with *that*?

As she contemplated, Marco did a brilliant job guiding her mom's spy toward the spinach prosciutto croissant—which was heavenly today, if Claire did say so herself—and then he got her to order an éclair to boot. Then he threw in a pitch for his olive loaf, which the lady pounced on, as she should.

"I just hope it's as good as you make it sound," she said with a slight lift of her eyebrows that could be considered slightly flirtatious.

"It will be," Marco promised warmly.

Was her mother matchmaking for Marco now too? That nearly set Claire off all over again.

Oh! She could throw together a creamy bacon pasta dish easily with the leftover macaroni noodles from the salad she'd made this morning. Her mom had taught her how to substitute cream for cheese to make the sauce richer, and it would be a great thing to offer the Wandering Gourmet.

Claire dashed over to Bow Tie, but when he glanced up, somehow it seemed as if he was looking down at her, and she freaked out a little.

"Would you like a pastry?" she squawked.

No, creamy bacon pasta was supposed to be coming out of her mouth. What was wrong with her?

Eric.

That was the answer to everything that was wrong with her and then some.

Worse, she was blowing it with Bow Tie. He got this disgusted look on his face and said, "I think I've had quite enough."

"Great," she muttered and pasted on a smile. "Perhaps I could refill your coffee."

"No. I'm done." He punctuated that with a snooty smirk. "Thank you."

How he managed to make those two words sound completely ungrateful was a mystery to her. "Okay."

Time to cut her losses. She hop-skipped back behind the counter where it was safe, but not before she saw Bow Tie immediately write something down in his notebook. *Chef is a scatterbrain and doesn't like to walk while indoors,* likely.

Marco ambushed her the second she sprang into the kitchen.

"You think that's him?"

"Yeah. Bow tie. Arrogance. Gotta be him."

Marco nodded once, his expression a bit grim, but really they'd done everything they could. The chips would have to fall where they fell. Or whatever the saying was. It certainly wasn't like she could count on fate to do anything of value for her.

Marco went back out front to hold down the fort. As she pulled a pan of croissants from the oven—not burned this time, thank goodness—she heard Marco's voice float back to her.

"Did Claire know you were coming in?"

Eric or her mother had walked in the door, she'd bet money. She shut her eyes for fortification until she heard the soft feminine response.

"Probably not."

Her mom, then.

Sure enough, here came the woman herself, barging into the kitchen to take over again.

"You weren't answering your phone," her mother said in the world's worst case of *no duh*.

There was a very good reason for that. Claire didn't want to talk to her mother. The nerve of her showing up at Gilded Sweets like everything was okay. It wasn't.

"So," her mom continued like they were having a perfectly fine discussion that she had every right to initiate. "I thought I'd just drop by."

"I really don't have time for this right now, Mom."

And frankly, she didn't think she could find a way to have time for any of her mother's shenanigans ever again.

Twenty

HER MOTHER, NEVER ONE TO take a hint even a little bit, followed Claire out into the dining room, still talking.

"I'm so sorry, sweetheart," Helen said earnestly and kept on trucking right over to the table Claire had started wiping down. "Can you ever forgive me?"

That deserved a response. Just not the one her mother probably wanted. "You need to let me live my own life."

"I know. I will," Helen insisted.

"You've said this before, and yet here we are."

Claire nearly knocked a glass bowl off the table in her blind haste to pretend this conversation wasn't upsetting her to the nth degree. But it was. They'd had variations of this conversation so many times, and her mother *never listened.*

"This time I mean it. I promise." Her mother's spine snapped straight as she swiped a hand through the air. "No more meddling, no more blind dates. I really think Eric is the one."

Claire slammed the plate in her hand against the table with far more force than she'd meant to, drawing the attention of every customer in the place. Miraculously, the earthenware dish didn't break. Unlike her heart.

"Your promise is barely ten seconds old," she cried. "And already you're giving me your opinion."

Her mother set down her coat and purse in a nearby chair, presumably so she could start the hard sell. "Claire, I'm sorry, but I believe in love and marriage and happily ever after! And I just want that for you."

"So do I!" She shut her eyes and breathed in slowly, then continued with a touch lower volume, "I want that too. But I need to find it on my own."

Like she'd been saying for umpteen years in eleventy billion different ways. Eric might well have been the one, but her mother had ruined any chance of allowing that to happen naturally by sticking her nose into it.

There was only one way to drive this home for Helen, and Claire didn't plan to pull any punches, not anymore.

"Okay. What if your mom had handpicked Dad? It would have taken the romance right out of it. I need to make my own mistakes. I need to find my own way."

And her mother took it exactly as if Claire had smacked her right between the eyes, her expression crumpling. "I...never realized..."

"That you are *pushing me away*." Claire finished

for her. "It's like you don't trust that I can handle my own life."

It looked like her mother was about to cry, but it was too hard for Claire to tell since her own eyes stung with unshed tears. This was the crux of the issue, the thing she couldn't see a way past. If her mother didn't get this now, she never would.

"That's not true," her mom said softly. "It's just my way of hanging on. Not just to you. But to me. The mom you go shopping with. The one you call when you need to share a secret or need encouragement. The mom you *need*. Not this woman. The one who's about to retire from who she used to be."

Oh, goodness. That was the most unfiltered thing her mom had ever said to her.

Claire let it roll around inside her. It softened everything, totally against her will.

And she saw the whole thing differently, in a light she'd never considered before. That of a mom losing her identity.

No wonder everything had gone all sideways. Her mom was struggling with the changes in her own life and badly bumbling their relationship as a result.

Something shifted in Claire's heart, resettling in a slightly different spot, but it was enough.

"You're always going to be my mother." *That* was the crux of the issue, the thing *Claire* needed to get. Maybe she already had, judging by the way her heart felt lighter and mushier all at once. "And I'm always going to need you. Even if you drive me crazy."

They both laughed softly, and her mother gave her a tender smile. "Are we still allowed to hug?"

Surprisingly, Claire wasn't mad anymore. All of it had drained away. "Yes."

"I'm sorry, sweetheart," her mother murmured in her ear, which didn't help the waterworks her eyeballs had turned into.

"It's okay."

And it was. Somehow. Chalk it up to a Gilded Sweets miracle.

Helen was her mother, good, bad, and everything in between. She loved her mom, and her mother loved her. Period. There was no other way to think about it.

And mostly, her mom had great taste in everything. Clothes, shoes, napkins. Men.

After all, she'd picked Claire's father. And Eric.

Not that she was in a big hurry to forgive him. But certain facts couldn't be denied, purely from an objective standpoint. Eric was a great guy on paper.

Too bad nothing about them was real. Not the romance of their meeting, not the romance of a kiss by candlelight. She didn't even feel like she knew him all that well at this point. Her best bet was to start the hard work of getting over him and moving on.

Why was she still thinking about him, then?

As her mother released her, the dark-haired lady she'd tagged as a friend of her mom's caught her gaze and smiled, clearly having overheard everything. She set down her cell phone deliberately. Claire wouldn't have been surprised to learn the woman had been the one to alert her mother whether Claire seemed receptive to a visit or not.

Marco buzzed over to the lady with her order, his attention clearly on the sideshow that had unfolded in full view of the customers. In full damage control mode, he set down the plate with flourish.

"Here you go. Let me know if you need anything else," he called loudly, trying to reset the atmosphere back into the realm of Professional Bakery instead of an episode of As the Éclair Turns.

"No, I'm fine. Can I ask you a question?" The woman glanced over at Claire and her mom, then up at Marco. "Is there always so much drama in here?"

Ouch. That was a little uncalled for, especially since it was highly likely the dark-haired woman had been involved somehow. Claire wanted to rush over and tell her no, this was highly unusual, and do it loud enough for everyone else to hear.

But before she could, Marco nodded.

"You have no idea," he told her, the big traitor.

But Claire had to smile. At least she and her mom were on the mend. And the Wandering Gourmet, if it had been Bow Tie, had thankfully missed all of the shenanigans. If her mother's spy had somehow assisted in the timing of that, great.

Otherwise, she'd chalk it up to fate still having its hand on Claire's life, for which she sent up a silent thank you as she jetted back to the kitchen to do some actual baking for once. Maybe fate had a few more surprises in store for her still.

Donna took her sweet time organizing the sheaf of papers Eric had handed her. She had something on her mind this morning, he'd wager, and she didn't make him wait too long before she got her mom face on.

"Have you talked to Claire?" she asked point blank, like he'd been the one to fail at contacting her.

He shook his head. "She's not answering her phone—not when I call, anyway. I went by the bakery instead, and that...did not go well."

The ache inside never quite went away, either. He'd hoped they could talk and he could figure out a way to tell her all the things he should have said from the beginning. But she'd been pretty clear that she didn't want anything to do with him.

"So, you're just not going to work on fixing this between you two?" Donna glanced over her shoulder as he slammed the copier lid a little harder than he'd meant to.

"I'm not sure there's much to fix." A little taken aback by the woman's firm tone, he leafed through the papers the copier had spit out, trying to sort out the jumble in his head. "But maybe it's for the best. I'll just throw all my energy into my work for a while."

Then he wouldn't have to think about how devastated Claire had looked as she'd walked away. Or how much he missed her. What was he supposed to do, though? Force her to talk to him?

"No," Donna countered immediately. "That's a bad idea. You have to call her."

Oh, well, why didn't he think of that? Had she purposefully tuned out everything he'd said? "Unfortunately, I think that ship has sailed."

"You need to stop feeling sorry for yourself and just call her," Donna said in that tone of voice that told him it was not a suggestion. "Or she will move on."

If she hadn't already. The thought made him queasy.

What would one more shot hurt? She wouldn't answer anyway.

Except she did.

"Hey," Claire said into the phone after not even letting it ring all that long. Almost as if she'd been expecting him to call.

"Um…hey," he repeated like a moron, fumbling around for some other words that weren't *hey*, but she'd thrown him for a giant loop. "Uh, look. I was just hoping we could talk."

Smooth move. Now she'd just say, *we're talking right now.*

But she didn't. "I don't know."

Which was better than no.

"One cup of coffee. That's all I ask." Even that would be more than he'd had five minutes ago. "You have to let me explain. Claire. Please."

"Okay."

Okay? As in *yes*? He barely stopped himself from dancing a little jig right there in the hallway between the copy room and the break room. But he restrained himself, because Nate had walked by and he'd make some kind of comment that would pull Eric off this amazing high.

Claire cleared her throat. "I'll meet you in an hour at that place near your office."

That was definitely an affirmative. He settled for an emphatic fist pump in lieu of the dancing. "Okay. Great."

But as soon as he ended the call, he let out a very heartfelt, "*Yes!*" that Donna must have overheard, because she smiled her knowing smile and disappeared to the front of the office to sign in a patient.

He'd give her credit for that one all day long.

The next hour dragged along until he thought he'd come unglued. Instead of continuing to drive himself nuts, he went to the coffee shop a bit early and caught up on his email while he waited for Claire.

Someone brushed by him in a cloud of feminine perfume and slid into the empty seat. Not Claire. *Dana*. Not dressed in her doctor clothes. In fact, she was wearing more makeup than usual and had done something different with her dark hair that gave her a more stylish look.

"Mind if I join you?" she asked. A moot point, since she'd already done so.

Startled, he glanced outside, praying Claire hadn't arrived yet. That was all he needed: for her to see him with Dana, who was clearly dressed to impress, and assume the worst. This was what happened when hanging out at a place close to the hospital. Unwanted companions.

"Dana. I'm sorry. But I'm waiting for someone."

That was her cue to get up and leave. As fast as possible. But she didn't. She toyed with the napkin on the table in front of her, biting her lip.

"Oh, okay. I just wanted to make something clear. I can be a little removed, but I'm interested, Eric. In case it doesn't show."

Wow. He hadn't seen that one coming. Nor was he the slightest bit interested in return. His heart belonged to Claire, hook, line, and sinker.

That was the first moment when he really internalized what he might've lost if Claire hadn't been willing to give him a chance to explain—*everything*. Claire was more important to him than anything else. When had that happened?

"Dana." He cleared his throat. "I'm seeing someone. And she's going to be here. Any minute."

And it would be most beneficial if Dana wasn't here.

Too late. Claire strolled right by the window where he sat with Dana, her gaze meeting his through the plate glass, then sliding to Dana. Eyes widening, Claire stuck her hands in her pockets and kept walking. Hopefully to the door of the coffee shop and not to continue on down the street.

"Oh," Dana said and finally got out of Claire's seat. "Is it serious?"

"It is for me," he told her truthfully. "Yeah."

"Okay." Dana glanced behind him and her expression indicated that Claire had indeed come inside the shop, because she'd immediately sized her up and dismissed her all in one shot. "Good luck."

They passed each other, and it was odd how there was no comparison between the two. They were both beautiful, accomplished women, but Dana faded away next to Claire.

"Hey," Claire said as she leaned a hip on the table, not quite committed to taking Dana's vacated chair apparently. "Who was that?"

"A doctor I work with. Dana."

The truth, but certainly not the whole truth or even very much truth, because he barely crossed paths with her on a regular basis. In fact, this was the first time he'd seen her since that night at the Chameleon.

"Well, based on the look she just gave me, I assume she's more than just a colleague."

She'd seen that too, had she? *Great.*

"Are you two dating?" Claire asked point-blank.

"No," he told her emphatically. "I mean, we did. But it's a thing of the past."

"Oh. You were with her when you met my mother."

This conversation had veered so far from the one he'd wanted to have that he couldn't get his feet under him. "Your mom told you I was on a date that night?"

Why would she do that? It painted him in the worst light possible.

Claire gave a little noise of disgust. "This was a bad idea."

"Look," he said a touch desperately, but he'd long passed the point of caring how transparent he was with his feelings. "We went out a couple of times but that's it. It's just you now, I promise."

Which shouldn't even be in question. He should've told her how he felt a thousand times already, right after he'd told her the truth about how he'd found her.

He felt his chance sliding away as her expression closed in.

"Claire, please—"

"Eric, I'm sorry." She shrugged once. "I'm sorry."

And then she left. He didn't go after her. What would he say? Nothing but a repeat of the arguments Claire had already rejected. And his heart was hurting too much at the moment to go through that again.

Twenty-One

"WE GOT IT," MARCO CALLED as he charged down the pier to interrupt Claire's solitude, the first time he'd done so in the two days since giving Eric another shot had imploded.

Just as well. She'd allowed herself twenty minutes of moping over Eric and then she'd planned to make herself stop. Which hadn't gone so well. Because here she was. Still moping.

Claire shoved off the railing to stand up straight. Leaning over the water was her favorite way to think, but it lacked a certain something when your love life had fallen apart.

Marco held out his phone, pointing at it. "We got a review."

"What?" she squeaked. Of all the things she'd expected him to say, that wasn't it. "What does it say?"

"I don't know. My buddy texted me the link. I'm just bringing it up now."

She crowded up next to Marco, the breeze off Lake Union pulling at her hair and draping it over the phone as he tapped. Then he handed it to her, squeezing his eyes shut, clearly unable to look himself.

"The Wandering Gourmet" marched across the top of the small screen. She glanced at Marco as her pulse pounded in her throat. This was it. Make-or-break time.

She paged down and started reading aloud. "'Gilded Sweets Bakery is a new entry into the overcrowded category of little luncheonettes.' That's not a very good start."

"Well, just keep reading."

Marco, the encouraging one? What was this world coming to? But dutifully, she let her eyes trail to the next part. "'But this little place is a...gem.'"

Her gaze collided with Marco's as the words settled into her chest. His dawning expression of wonder must match her own.

"We're a hit!" he exclaimed, which widened her own smile.

"He likes us," she breathed, hardly able to fathom what was happening.

Marco curled two fingers toward himself and repeated in a *gimme* motion. "Let me read."

She handed him the phone and stuck her head over his shoulder to follow along.

"'The olive bread was the real thing,'" he said so carefully that it almost brought tears to her eyes. "'Made with enormous skill.'"

She was so pleased for him. "Aww, your father's recipe."

"And his father before him." Marco kissed his fingers and threw them toward the sky in deference to his late forebearers. "Papa."

"He'd be very proud," she told him. "Okay. 'The delicate croissant filled with spinach and prosciutto was a delightful surprise.' But wait. He didn't order that, did he?"

Of course, it was possible she misremembered. She did have Eric on the brain twenty-four seven lately.

"No." Marco snapped his fingers. "But I know who did. The Wandering Gourmet is a woman."

Claire grinned. "Oh. Well, that would explain the good taste."

Thrilled to the marrow, Claire started strolling down the boardwalk along the waterfront, scrolling through the review to get to the part she hadn't read yet. "'The chocolate éclair was beyond compare, traditional, but complex. My compliments to the chef.'"

That would be me. She pressed her hand to her chest.

"Yes, yes, very nice." Marco grabbed his phone to see what else the Wandering Gourmet had to say. "Okay. *Okay.* 'The ambience is equally appealing, and the owners provided wonderful drama, both in and out of the kitchen.'"

"Oh, my mom is going to like that."

All at once, everything snapped into place with a final click. Her mother's spy! Who probably wasn't a spy in retrospect, since she'd been the only person in the place during the great mother-daughter showdown who'd also ordered the spinach prosciutto.

And the whole time, Claire had assumed the dark-haired woman was her mom's friend. Why had she thought that, again?

The gallery. That was where she'd seen the lady before.

Fate was still on her side. The gallery catering gig might've been the reason Gilded Sweets had landed on the Wandering Gourmet's radar. *Thanks, Mom*.

Who would have thought fate could work so well together with Helen the Puppet Master?

Claire wasn't sure she should tell her mom, though. It would only encourage her bad behavior. But the review was so good and felt like such an answered prayer that she couldn't be upset the Wandering Gourmet had witnessed the scene between Claire and her mother.

Marco kept reading. "'I give this wonderful bakery a very enthusiastic *four stars*!'"

No. Way. *No way*. She might have screamed a little. But four stars? For Gilded Sweets?

"That's the highest rating," Marco shouted and picked her up to spin her around so fast that her head spun. "We did it, we did it, we did it."

He set her down, and she high-fived him, still shrieking with joy. "I'm so proud of us."

She was still on that high when they opened the doors of the bakery. And she needed the adrenaline burst, because holy cow, did that review bring in the crowds. They were lined up at the counter four and five deep, opening their wallets for boxes of goodies and bread, jostling for tables to eat in.

It was fabulous.

Marco darted back and forth behind Claire, who was manning the register, only pausing long enough to mutter in her ear, "We're going to have to get more tables."

"And more staff," she murmured back and then smiled as she handed a man four coconut lime tarts. "Thank you."

Marco reached over her to grab the last croissant. "Maybe we can buy the place next door."

"Now you want to spend money," she said with mock incredulity. It was a thought. She stuck two baguettes in a bag and gave them to the next customer. "Thank you so much."

They were *so* busy. The good kind of busy, the kind that made her so happy her cheeks hurt from smiling. They'd done it. They'd really created something worthwhile with Gilded Sweets, and now everyone knew about it.

The only blemish on what was otherwise a stellar day was the fact that she couldn't call Eric to tell him the news. He'd have been thrilled for her.

But that wasn't how things had turned out. Eric wasn't in her life anymore, and that was that.

On his next trip behind Claire, Marco commented with a sense of wonder, "I'm almost out of olive bread. I'm going to have to get baking."

The magic of a good review. They were almost out of everything the Wandering Gourmet had name-checked in her column. It was unbelievable. The customers kept Claire hopping, so much so that she scarcely had time to think about Eric. Thankfully.

She had a strong suspicion he'd creep back into her thoughts eventually, though.

And then she wouldn't be able to get him out again.

The feast Helen had cooked rivaled any restaurant in existence—except Claire's—and Sam ate the first bite of her carbonara with gusto. "Honey, this is delicious."

His wife smiled. At him. Something she did a lot lately.

"I wanted to make something really special."

"What's the occasion?"

"Let's just say I've turned over a new leaf. From this point on, I plan on letting things unfold without my involvement."

Sure. He'd heard that one before. "Does Claire know about this?"

"She's the one who gave me my marching orders. So I'm to get on with my life and let her get on with hers."

The words sounded like the right ones, but not coming out of his wife's mouth. She'd still be trying to arrange her own funeral even after she'd taken her last breath. But that was what he loved about her. She knew what she wanted and went after it with all her energy. Like when she'd decided she wanted him.

He'd never have thought that finding out the truth

about their first meeting would actually end up making him feel even more special.

If Helen really had changed her stripes, he'd eat his socks instead of this carbonara, but far be it from him to argue the point when Helen so clearly believed it was true this time.

"She's a wise woman, that daughter of yours," he said mildly.

"If she and Eric ever get together," she mused softly, "that would be great."

That was more like the woman he knew and loved. But he couldn't help giving her a look designed to show that he was on to her.

She lifted her hands in surrender, easily interpreting his thoughts despite him not voicing them. "From now on, her love life is none of my business. But who I love is up to me. How's the carbonara?"

Sam recognized a subject change if he'd ever heard one and indulged her because that was what he did, making noises of appreciation as he loved his wife the best way he knew possible—by pretending her faults didn't exist. "I mean, only the Italians would think of putting bacon and eggs on pasta."

"Those Italians think of everything," Helen agreed.

"We'll have to go there sometime."

He was joking. But it was nice to be able to, when Italy had been such a touchy subject for so long.

Helen didn't laugh, though. She put her fork down and gave him this cryptic look that had him second-guessing whether they were at a place where he could crack jokes about Italy.

"Ready for dessert?" she asked brightly.

He glanced down at his half-full plate. "We just started dinner."

"I can't wait," she said and slid from her chair to dash into the kitchen as he shoveled two bites into his mouth in rapid succession, since it didn't appear he'd get a chance to enjoy the rest.

She waltzed back to the table with a long plate of pastries and set it on the table. "Cappuccino cannoli, a present from Claire. And here is a little something from me."

She handed him a blue folder, which he took with curiosity. "What is this?"

But she shrugged with that cryptic smile again, forcing him to open it to find out what the big mystery was. The rectangular pieces of paper tucked inside threw him back a few years, before the advent of the digital age, but he recognized what they were immediately.

A peace offering. The beginning of the second chapter of their lives. Everything he wanted wrapped up in these little pieces of paper.

Drawing them out, he held them up and glanced at her with a broad smile. "Two tickets to Venice."

"And then Tuscany, then the coast. Then, wherever you want to go, Mr. Michaels."

Laughing with undisguised glee, he took her hand. This meant everything to him.

"I don't care where I go. As long as you're beside me." He lifted his glass with his free hand and touched the rim to hers. "Mrs. Michaels."

This was going to be the best period of their entire lives. He could feel it in his bones, and he'd never been happier to have reached this milestone with Helen. Miraculously, she seemed to be on that page now, too. As if she'd figured out that spending more time together wasn't the death sentence she'd been treating it as.

And another plus—it would be harder to meddle in Claire's life from Italy.

Somehow, he knew his wife would find a way, though.

Once her parents had committed to Italy, a bon voyage party had been a necessity. Claire invited her whole family to the bakery, giving up precious table space to all her cousins, Uncle Arnie, and a few of her mom's friends. Her father hadn't stopped talking about the trip and had launched into another recital of their itinerary.

"And then, we finish the trip in Florence," he said to the table at large with a flourish.

Jill piped up from across the table. "I can't believe you guys are leaving so soon."

"Yep." Sam gave her mom a secret smile, full of all their years together, that made Claire's heart feel like it would burst. "One week from tomorrow."

Helen put a hand on Sam's arm. "I almost wish we were there already."

Claire set a platter on the table near her dad's arm

and turned the seven-layer cake toward her parents. She'd spent hours making this so it would be perfect, and she couldn't wait to serve it to them. They deserved all the happiness she could see reflected on their faces.

And she wasn't jealous at all. Very much, anyway. Okay, maybe more than she'd let on. But they made it look so easy to have relationship issues and yet still piece it all back together.

Why couldn't her own love life come together like that? She'd tried to stay positive after the Eric Disaster, but it was as if fate had decided Claire wasn't going to get a happily ever after, and there was no way to force it to budge on the matter.

"Claire, that's beautiful," her mother exclaimed over the cake.

"*Viaggio sicuro*," she said.

"'Bon voyage,'" her dad translated in case there was anyone at the table who couldn't figure that out on their own.

From the corner of her eye, she spied Marco as he came around the counter to shake the hand of a dark-haired lady, and when she turned her head, Claire realized it was the Wandering Gourmet.

Holy cow! The Wandering Gourmet had come back to Gilded Sweets. How much of an endorsement was *that*?

Claire smiled at her mother as she sliced off a piece of cake to serve to her, straining to hear the conversation in case the Wandering Gourmet had changed her glowing opinion about the bakery.

"Hi," Marco said to her enthusiastically. "I just wanted to thank you for that lovely review."

"Oh, no thanks necessary. You deserved it," the lady said. "Just promise me you won't give away my identity."

"No problem. I'm just happy to see you," Marco said with a touch more texture than might have been obligatory when speaking to a food critic. "Looks like you're becoming a regular."

Duh moment. Maybe the Wandering Gourmet wasn't here for the food. She and Marco were standing oh-so close to each other. The other day, there had been a distinct vibe between them that didn't seem to have fizzled.

How lovely would that be if Marco and the Wandering Gourmet hit it off?

"Are you kidding me?" The lady flipped a hand in Claire's direction. "This is the best show in town."

Okay, well maybe there was another reason the bakery had gained popularity. Claire would give her that one. But with Claire's parents on the way to Italy, there wasn't going to be much drama around here anymore.

"Yes," Marco agreed readily. "Claire's life is very entertaining."

She rolled her eyes and turned back to her family, letting Marco have his "moment" with the Wandering Gourmet.

"And it looks like another show is about to begin," he continued.

What was that supposed to mean? Then she did

a double take when she noticed Marco staring at the doorway. She turned around in slow motion, pretty certain she knew what she'd see.

Eric.

She stood there staring at him, silently begging her heart to stop twisting around so painfully. For crying out loud, why did the sight of him still affect her so much?

He was just so...everything. Still that guy who had convinced her to take pastries to a scared little girl in the hospital. Still that guy who had hung out with her in the kitchen all those times when she couldn't make a date due to an unexpected catering job she'd desperately needed to take.

"Eric, please don't do this," she told him, her voice breaking, which probably told him everything he needed to know about what was going on inside her. "I'm trying to get over you."

He spread his arms, not letting her look away. "How do you get over what's meant to be?"

What was he talking about? "I thought you didn't believe in destiny."

"I don't," he said succinctly.

Right. Cold calculation was his jam. Everything happened according to design, leaving no room for the magic of romance. They weren't compatible and never would be.

"Then what are you doing here?"

"I'm here for you," he said simply, moving closer, crowding into her space, into her thoughts. "And I'm here for us."

Okay, that had sounded pretty romantic, almost as if he'd come here to sweep her off her feet.

"Come on, Claire," she heard Marco murmur behind her. "Meet him halfway."

Oh, she wanted to. She wanted to believe that everything she'd ever wanted could be right here within her reach if she'd simply hold out her hand. But how could she?

She'd had all these ideas about what her perfect, magical fairy-tale romance would look like, and reality wasn't anything close.

Everything was all messed up.

"Look," Eric said. "You can call it fate or a mother's intuition or a coincidence that brought us together. But it doesn't matter how we got here, because all I know is that I love you. And I don't ever want to lose you again."

Her heart filled all at once, and she couldn't look away from the tender expression on his face. He meant every word. She could tell. If nothing else, she believed that the man he'd been with her every day since the gallery was the real deal.

And he was standing here, begging her to take a chance on love instead of holding out for a chance meeting with someone else that might never happen.

Was this the surprise fate had in store for her? To fall in love with the man who'd been put in her path not by accident but by her mother?

Helen sniffled and called out, "Would you just kiss her already?"

Amid the scattered laughter of the very large audience, Eric stepped closer, taking Claire into his arms. She didn't resist. Nor did she want to. The moment he touched her, she knew. It was silly to hold out for a different fairy tale when the only one she wanted was right here. Within reach.

"Should we make her wait?" he asked.

"She can wait," Claire murmured. "But I can't."

When he kissed her, something inside broke open, and Eric rushed in to replace whatever she might have lost. As it should be. Because he was perfect for her. It didn't matter how they'd met. What mattered was how they spent every day from now on.

The kiss went on and on as the entire bakery full of people broke out into applause. That was enough to remind Claire she was at work in full view of her family and customers. She and Eric had plenty of time to explore every aspect of their newfound love.

She pulled away, but Eric didn't let her get too far.

"You're so romantic," she told him through happy tears.

How lucky was she?

Epilogue

AN IMPROMPTU TOUR OF CAPRI turned out to be the best part of Helen's Wednesday.

Tomorrow, Sam would come up with something else wonderful. That was what he'd done every day of their semi-permanent vacation, while she'd spent most of hers trying to make it up to him for taking so long to get on a plane to Italy.

The Mediterranean had turned this cerulean color that spread out as far as the eye could see. Helen stood at the railing of the ferry boat that motored toward the island of Capri just off the coast of Sorrento, letting the breeze tear at her hair.

When they'd first arrived in Venice, she'd done a lot of damage control to her hairstyle, then eventually moved to wearing one of several exquisite silk scarves she'd picked up in Florence, which they'd decided to visit second instead of as the grand finale. The scarves had lasted all of a week. Then she realized she didn't care that much about maintaining a professional appearance.

Italy was all about experiences. Not presentation.

Sam joined her at the railing, his warm hand covering hers.

"You up for seeing the Blue Grotto?" he asked with a smile as he held up two printed tickets, fanning them with a flick of his wrist. "I booked us an excursion."

He was so handsome and just so *it* that her pulse fluttered. Still. After all these years, he could affect her by doing nothing more than standing there. "Sounds amazing."

Everything did. All the time. She'd even gained a few pounds, as she'd predicted, but somehow, she didn't care. Neither did Sam.

"I figure it's a great last hoo-rah before we pack it in," he said. "Maybe tomorrow or the next day, we can drive up the coast to Rome and catch a flight to the States."

"What?" Her heart did a giant swan dive and splatted right into the Mediterranean. "What do you mean, catch a plane? You want to cut our trip short?"

Madness. Had she missed something in the grand scheme of things? Surely Sam was having the time of his life, the same as she was.

Sam stared at her. "Honey, we said two months. It's been two. Don't you want to go home? You were just saying you miss Claire."

The words didn't compute. "It can't possibly have been two months already."

But then, Helen couldn't recall the last time she'd looked at a calendar. She pulled her phone from her purse and glanced at the date. Huh. He wasn't wrong.

He gave her an indulgent smile. "I'll take it as a positive that you're not tired of my company yet."

"I could never get tired of you," she told him playfully. "Or this view."

Since she had her phone in her hand, she clicked off a series of pictures and sent the best one to Eric on the sly with the accompanying text: *Wish you were here.*

Her daughter's boyfriend always sent back a smiley face or a short comment to the effect of *beautiful* or *wow*. No clue as to whether he'd actually mentioned something to Claire about traveling to Italy for a few days, the big lug. Surely, he could take a hint.

She wouldn't push her luck, though. Not after promising Claire that she'd butt out of her love life. No one could fault her for sending a few perfectly innocent vacation pictures though, right?

"I do miss Claire," she said honestly. "But there's no reason to rush home, is there?"

"What are you saying? You want to stay?" Sam pulled her away from the railing to square her hips so she was facing him, then searched her face. "What about getting back to your clients? I thought this was just a short trip to tide us over until you were ready to permanently retire."

"Maybe I'm ready."

Saying it out loud didn't send a rush of panic through her chest like she would've expected. All she knew was that she didn't want to leave Italy with all of the art and rolling hills yet to be discovered. They hadn't ventured far enough north to hit Lake Como and it would be practically criminal to jet home without seeing the Alps.

Plus, she liked having nothing to focus on but Sam. Well, that and her campaign to get Eric and Claire on a plane. There was no better place to propose to a woman than Italy.

Honestly, what was wrong with Eric that he hadn't taken her hints already? If it wasn't for her, that couple would never get anywhere.

"Ready?" Sam repeated as if she'd started speaking Swahili. "You mean you're serious? You want to make retirement a permanent deal?"

She shrugged, not sure what it said about the situation that he was so shocked. "I've been having a great time. Haven't you?"

"Sure, but I just don't know what to say." Sam shook his head. "I had kind of gotten myself prepared to go back home."

"Is that what you want?"

The chug of the ferry engine pulling into the dock at Capri filled the silence as he contemplated for only a split second. "I mean, I miss Claire, too. But this is our life, our time to do what makes us happy. And I love everything about Italy."

"So do I." She touched his cheek with two fingers. "And that's entirely too serious of a face for a man whose wife told him she's ready to retire permanently after all."

Sam let a grin spill onto his face. And then he did something totally spontaneous by picking her up and spinning her around as if they were still twenty with the world at their feet.

Well, what did age matter? The world was still at their feet and now they had the freedom to explore it.

"Helen Michaels," he said as he sat her down. "You are the most amazing woman on the planet. I would like to stay."

"No end date, okay?"

"Deal." But then he sobered a bit. "We'll have to figure out what to do with the house now that we're not going home."

"Claire can do some winterizing and extend the contract with the lawn maintenance people," Helen said easily.

There wasn't anything she didn't know about taking care of an empty house. This would be the first time doing it on her own property instead of a client whose house hadn't sold, though. It felt a little surreal. But good. The best kind of transition.

The ferry docked, and people began spilling out onto the sun-drenched isle of Capri. Sam took Helen's hand and they strolled along Via Cristoforo Columbo from the terminal, content to have no agenda other than to catch a boat later to the Blue Grotto.

Sam paused in front of one shop, turning to look back out over the terrain. "I had the vague sense that we were going up in elevation, but wow. Look at that view."

She followed his gaze, her breath catching as the port and then the sparkling Mediterranean spread out quietly below them. "Amazing. Maybe we should stay here for a while."

"You don't want to go back to Venice?"

A fair question. That city with the romantic gondolas and history seeping from the cobblestones had so captured her that she'd made a comment about staying there forever. And Tuscany had its pluses too, with the stellar wineries and patchwork-patterned hills.

But Capri held the distinction of being the last place she'd sent a picture of to Eric. It made logical sense that if he did catch a clue and hustle her daughter onto a plane, he'd bring Claire here. Which she couldn't tell Sam straight out, not without him lecturing her.

Yes, she knew she'd promised to stay out of Claire's life, but this was different! Helen wasn't trying to play matchmaker anymore. Now she was just trying to get a ring on her daughter's finger before Helen died of old age, not ever having had a chance to help Claire plan a wedding. Or that brief moment when Helen would get to play mother of the bride.

Not to mention grandchildren.

That settled it. There were no two ways about it. People who left that kind of important stuff to fate had no idea what it took to actually make things happen. Fortunately for Claire, her mother wasn't one of them.

"Maybe we stay in Capri for a little while," she said casually as she took out her phone for one more quick picture and furtive text message. "And go back to Venice in a few weeks. The world is our oyster, Mr. Michaels."

He smiled. "Indeed it is, Mrs. Michaels."

Fate had seen fit to rain down success on Gilded Sweets at the same time Claire had finally figured out her love life. Irony at its finest. The more she just wanted to spend time with Eric, the busier the bakery got.

Even after hiring three new servers, she and Marco could barely keep up with the demand. It was the happiest kind of exhausted you could get.

Eric was a champ about it though, doing exactly what he'd always done—hang around the kitchen late at night as she worked on prepping things for the next day. Tonight was no exception. Despite a long day at the hospital mentoring some new pediatricians, here he was at the long silver table, cracking jokes and generally making her feel like all her dreams had come true.

"I have a present for you," he said and pulled something out from behind an industrial bag of flour, which Marco must've helped him hide.

Claire dusted off her hands and took the large box from Eric with a quizzical glance times two—one for the box and one for him. "It's not my birthday."

"Does it need to be?" he shot back with a sly grin. "Open it."

She tore through the tape in record time and lifted

out…a globe. "Thanks? Just what the owner of a bakery needs."

He laughed at her sarcasm, not the least bit offended. "You already have all the baking dishes a chef could want. You've been so busy lately, I figured you needed a break in some vacation spot somewhere that will pamper you. And where you don't have to cook. Let me whisk you away where it's just the two of us."

That sounded lovely. Both the pampering and the whisking.

But how could she take the time right now? Flustered, she glanced around the back room of Gilded Sweets, which was frankly a disaster thanks to having zero opportunity to do much of anything other than bake and run the restaurant.

Not that she was complaining! Her life was perfect. Almost.

The thought of taking a few days away from it all—with Eric—nearly made her swoon. She wanted to do it so badly she could taste it.

Maybe they could jet to Los Angeles for a day or something.

"Where are we going?" she asked, just to test out the idea.

Too late. Eric's broad smile fluttered her insides, and if he kept that up, there would be actual swooning. Now she was committed. She couldn't disappoint him.

"That's up to you," he told her and held up the globe. "I wanted to surprise you with a romantic trip, but when I started making all the plans, it felt too calculated. I figured it was better to let fate decide."

Enchanted, she leaned forward and kissed him square on the mouth. He really got her. Every day, she woke up and thought it would be impossible to love him more than she had when she went to sleep, and every day, he proved her wrong.

"Spin," he instructed. "Close your eyes and let your finger drop. Fate hasn't steered us wrong so far."

She did as he asked, because how could she not? But when she opened her eyes, the familiar boot shape under her finger was all wrong. *Italy*. It was half a world away.

Although…her mother had called her earlier that day to announce that she and Claire's dad had decided to stay in Italy indefinitely. Wouldn't it be fun to surprise them? Just show up one day and be like, *"Hey, fancy meeting you here."*

She shut her eyes. She couldn't.

But maybe she could. Just for a few days. Marco would be okay with covering for her, she knew it.

"Looks like we're going to Italy," she told him. The look he gave her had her doing a double take. "What? That's where my finger landed. You saw it."

"I know, it's just…" He exhaled noisily. "Your parents are there and it feels like we're crowding them. Are you sure this is a good idea?"

"I miss my mom," she said honestly. "But Italy is a big place. We don't have to hang out with them or anything if you don't want to."

"Okay." He spread his hands. "This is your choice.

If you want to go to Italy, we're going to Italy. It's fate, right?"

"And who are we to second-guess fate?"

And that was how she ended up on a plane to Marco Polo Airport in Venice. With Eric, the love of her life, who was the absolute perfect man for her. He was kind, funny, a steady rock of reasonableness, while she tended to float away on a sea of dreams occasionally.

Venice was unbelievably gorgeous, drenched in history and color and culture. She couldn't believe the splendor that unfolded as they boarded a vaporetto to take them the rest of the way. Imagine—this was the Venetian equivalent of a taxi! There was water everywhere, though, and she couldn't stop smiling as they sped toward the city.

It wasn't until they got to the Hotel Danieli that she started to suspect Eric might be a mind reader. Or there was something else going on—something that had to do with the text messages he got occasionally that put a slight guilty expression on his face, which she'd ignored because she figured she was reading into it.

"I'm trying to decide if I'm supposed to be mad at you," she murmured after they'd checked in and the desk agent handed them each a key to their separate rooms.

"What? Why would you be mad?" Eric asked as he handed her luggage to the valet, who would wheel it to her room for her.

"I'm not sure," she muttered, though she'd bet her mother had something to do with whatever it was.

"Okay," Eric said brightly. "Let's get settled. Meet me downstairs in thirty minutes. There's something I want you to see."

She was downstairs in twenty.

No chance of missing whatever he'd gone to great lengths to arrange. This was her Italian adventure, and she couldn't wait to see what was in store for her.

Eric arrived in the lobby, looking gorgeous and a little harried as he hustled her out of the lobby and down the street to a beautiful area that overlooked the Grand Canal. The sun had started to set, throwing incredible colors into the sky. There were little lights woven through the wooden lattice work that covered the alcove, and it was so magical that she strained to see the fairies that had surely played a part in this tale.

Except there were no fairies. Just a very familiar-looking couple standing near the alcove holding hands.

"Claire!" her mother exclaimed and rushed forward to hug her, enveloping her in love and memories.

"You don't seem very surprised to see us," she said wryly as she hugged her dad. "Hi, Dad. You both look very happy."

Funny how they just happened to be here. In Venice. Near the same hotel.

They did look great though, rested, and her mother had on new clothes that she must've bought along the way. Italy agreed with them, and now that she was here, Claire could definitely see why they'd extended their stay.

"It's the food," her dad said with a nod at her mother. "She lets me eat whatever I want here."

Claire laughed and shoulder-checked Eric. "This is the big surprise? I could have guessed you'd somehow arrange to run into my parents. You and my mom are big texting buddies, after all."

And no, she wasn't mad. She'd even said she missed her mom. It was a nice gesture to have coordinated with her parents so she had a chance to see them. Eric had scored major points just now.

"That's not the surprise," he said with a mischievous grin. "That is."

She followed the line of his nod and gasped.

A gondola had glided into place below the alcove, and two costumed men held a big banner that read, "Claire Michaels, will you marry me?" A third burst into song, accompanying himself with a mandolin as Italian words poured out of his mouth, a heartbreaking and beautiful serenade all at the same time.

"What is all of this?" she exclaimed, but when she glanced at Eric, he'd kneeled down on one knee in front of her, holding out a ring that sparkled so much brighter than the fairy lights. But it was dim compared to the sunburst in her heart.

"Will you marry me?" he asked in his deep, rich voice that thrilled through her.

This was so crazy. They'd barely been dating for two months. But he'd gone to all of this trouble to set up this proposal, despite letting fate decide their destination, and the romance of it stole her breath. She was so overcome that she could barely speak.

He took her mute, shocked silence as an opportunity to pour out his heart.

"Claire, I've wanted to ask you to spend the rest of your life with me since the moment I saw you across that gallery," he said sincerely, throwing her back to that moment when she'd first seen him and just... *known* he was the one. "But my dumb science brain thought it made more sense to wait. I had to be sure, to weigh everything out, take all the romance out of it. It took you in my life to make me realize we can't wait for all the data before we grab onto happiness with both hands. Marry me, and let's discover together what else destiny has in store for us."

"Yes," she said clearly, and that was all her tight throat could get out around the giant lump that had formed.

It didn't matter. That one little word was apparently enough for Eric, who slid the ring on her finger and leaped to his feet to pull her into the most rib-crushing hug she'd ever experienced. The sound of clapping rang out from around them—they'd gathered a crowd of onlookers.

Let them look. This was her moment, and everything was perfect.

They were *engaged*. She'd get to plan a wedding with her mother, and at the end, she'd be married to Eric. Claire Carlton had a very nice ring to it.

"I thought for a second you were going to say no," he murmured in her ear. His heart pounded against hers, testifying to how worked up she'd gotten him over a little thing like a half-second's hesitation. "What tipped it for you?"

"The fact that you made sure to include my mom in your proposal," she told him with a laugh. "But I was never going to say no. I love you too much to let you get away."

"Same goes," he said and kissed her at last in what would go down as the best engagement story to tell her kids that she could imagine.

The End

Claire's Coconut Lime Tarts

A Hallmark Original Recipe

In *Love By Chance*, these tarts are a specialty at Claire's bakery. After she meets a handsome doctor named Eric at an art gallery fundraiser, they start dating... and he sends more customers her way. Claire and Eric just click, and she feels so lucky that they happened to meet. It must've been fate...or was it?

Yield: 6 servings
Prep Time: 25 minutes
Cook Time: 20 minutes
Total Time: 45 minutes

INGREDIENTS

Coconut Crumb Crust:
- 2½ cups coconut cookie crumbs, (crisp coconut cookies crushed in a food processor) or crushed graham cracker crumbs
- 3 tablespoons granulated sugar
- ½ cup + 2 tablespoons melted butter

Coconut-Lime Filling:
- 5 large egg yolks, lightly beaten
- ¼ cup fresh-squeezed lime juice
- 1 cup sweetened condensed milk
- ¼ cup cream of coconut (such as Coco Lopez or Coco Real)
- 1 tablespoon fresh grated lime zest

Topping:
- ¾ cup whipped cream
- 2 tablespoons shaved or shredded sweetened coconut
- 6 fresh-cut lime wedges

DIRECTIONS

1. Preheat oven to 350°F. Spray six 4-inch fluted tart pans or one 9-inch fluted tart pan with cooking spray.
2. To prepare coconut crumb crust: combine crushed cookie crumbs or graham cracker crumbs, sugar and butter in a bowl. Mix with

a fork until crumbs are evenly blended with butter.

3. Press crumbs evenly over the bottom and sides of each tart pan to form a ¼-inch thick crust. Arrange tart pans on a baking sheet and bake uncovered for 8 to 10 minute, or until golden. Remove from oven and cool.

4. To prepare coconut cream-lime tarts: combine egg yolks, lime juice, sweetened condensed milk and cream of coconut in the top pan of a double boiler; whisk until completely blended. Place over bottom half of double boiler, filled with simmering water. Cook over medium low-heat, whisking constantly, for about 5 minutes or until custard filling is steaming hot. Increase heat to medium and cook for about 5 minutes or until filling is starting to bubble, stirring frequently. Add lime zest and stir until blended.

5. Spoon filling evenly into prepared tart crusts. Refrigerate uncovered until tarts are completely chilled and filling is firm (about 4 to 6 hours).

6. To serve: top each chilled tart with a dollop of whipped cream, a sprinkle of shaved coconut and a lime wedge.

Thanks so much for reading *Love by Chance*. We hope you enjoyed it!

You might like these other books from Hallmark Publishing:

Moonlight in Vermont
The Secret Ingredient
Love on Location
Love Locks
A Dash of Love
Dater's Handbook

For information about our new releases and exclusive offers, sign up for our free newsletter at hallmarkchannel.com/hallmark-publishing-newsletter

You can also connect with us here:

Facebook.com/HallmarkPublishing

Twitter.com/HallmarkPublish

About the Author

Come for the romance, stay for the happily ever after. Kacy writes novels starring swoon-worthy heroes that you can share with your daughter, the ladies at church, and your grandmother without fear because her books never contain bad language, violence or adult content. She lives in Texas where she's seen bobcats and beavers near her house, but sadly, not one cowboy. She's raising two mini-ninjas alongside the love of her life who cooks while she writes, which is her definition of a true hero.